G.E.N.I.U.S. & Magic

John Rodat

Copyright © 2018 John Rodat

All rights reserved.

ISBN: 1986967980
ISBN-13: 978-1986967983

"If Sir Terry Pratchett and the Marquis de Sade had a child . . . well, let's face it, we should all be happy because that would represent a striking scientific advance, and who doesn't like science? But also, if that child were as hilarious as his father and as ribald as his . . . other father, he might be John Rodat. *G.E.N.I.U.S. and Magic* is a rip-roaring adventure in the great tradition of *Another Fine Myth* and *Fanny Hill: Memoirs of a Woman of Pleasure*."

- D.J. Butler, author of *Witchy Eye*

"*G.E.N.I.U.S. and Magic* satisfies by providing equal measures of both. This is the work of an unbridled, irreverent and very odd imagination. Option this one while it's still affordable."

-Robert Rodat, Oscar-nominated screenwriter of *Saving Private Ryan*, and the author's Uncle Bob

Lord Vadney Kimberly Carroll Poon-Grebe, the 13th Marquis d'Isle d'Eaux, took notes as he gazed across the dewy fields: The girl was 16, he guessed. Maybe 17. But so unlike the girls of similar age at court, in the city. Such girls were possessed of an awful precocious guile; so worldly, so knowing, so unrattled by Lord Vadney's most painstaking efforts at deviance. He recalled one young lady, the daughter of a baron, who had giggled lasciviously at the collection of decks of playing cards, all explicitly anatomically illustrated (his "Blue 52s," he called them), which he kept in a glass-topped display in his private rooms in his house in town. Giggled! Without so much as the slightest tint of blush on her powdered cheek! Without the tiniest flicker of trepidation! "Why, Lord Vadney," she cooed. "You've got the beginnings of a promising collection, here. You must someday view my own small gallery. Have you anything yet from the hill tribes of Mount Venus? I don't think they play cards but their beadwork is absolutely filthy!"

    The evening, Vadney recollected ruefully, had been an enormous disappointment. For a baron's daughter, she had proved surprisingly — aggressive. He had nearly ruined a perfectly fitted waistcoat as he slipped out the library window. Driven from one's own home! The morals of the younger generation of the city were quite shocking. Lord Vadney feared for the future. He was at times quite despondent thinking of his own shock at the unshockable youth of the capital. But here in the countryside, among the farm folk, the rustic stock, among the barmaids, the milkmaids, the . . . egg maids? Was that a thing? The marquis, despite his vast holdings in this region, was not well-versed in the life details of its inhabitants. He was not specifically aware of the degree of difference between this type of plump servant girl and that. Though this is not to say he was uninterested in them or their differences. He was, in fact quite keen to learn the differences — just not those specific to the particular chores assigned to them by their cooper fathers, blacksmith brothers, or poacher husbands. No, Lord Vadney Poon-Grebe was a rare connoisseur: a man with appetites both broad and deep, though uncommon. This much he had hinted, even stated outright — "I am a man with appetites both broad and deep, though uncommon." — to many a dinner guest, visiting diplomat, page, court alchemist, apothecary, drunken cleric, jester, barber and bonesetter in or just off his path. By now, he must have really quite a burgeoning notoriety, must haven't he? Must be regarded with a mixture of prurient curiosity, revulsion and respect, probably. I mean, if you had to guess. It'd be in that neighborhood, between evil Svengali and demi-demon, maybe.

A little eerie, anyway. Odd?

"Creep."

Well, no. Not "creep." Creep didn't have anywhere near the elegance, the nefarious punch, the murky appeal and invitation to depraved depths that he'd ...

"Oy! You! Creep!"

It was a surprisingly deep and powerful voice for a lass of only 16, maybe 17. There is a downside to the delightful heft of a farm-fed country girl. Lord Vadney tucked the notebook in which he'd been recording his thoughts about this startlingly voiced creature into his masterfully mended waistcoat, after drawing a line through the entire brief entry. He painfully jabbed himself in the hip with the small stylus and trudged — mysteriously, devilishly, said the voice in Vadney's head — back into the encroaching twilight that spawned him, falling only once and then into the night that spawned him.

 Mysteriously. Devilishly.

 Or as mysteriously and devilishly as allowed by the heavy boots upon which that dratted worrywart Ratch had insisted.

 Mysteriously. Devilishly.

 He trudged.

 Encroaching twilight.

 "Damn."

 Marchioness Camilla Fitz-Victim Poon-

John Rodat

Grebe cuddled her fat son, Nelson, on a divan of scrolled exotic wood and luxurious upholstery. The viewer is offered the description in hope of sparing him or her the embarrassment of an understandable misapprehension. It would be easy to mistake the aforementioned tableau for another: For example, a teak caravan built by colorblind gypsies transporting a powdered egret actively trying to consume a whole live hog in a command performance for an audience of just two — for Lady Poon-Grebe and Nelson were joined by the Viscountess De Louche, Lady Mary Anne Sauvignon, and Countess Hertz-Nuptial, Lady Prunella Mantiss (of whom, of course, you have heard). It is, perhaps, unlikely, that any would come to such conclusion but we seek to avoid any awkwardness, where possible.

"Egad!" cried Vadney, ducking into a closet. "Gypsies!"

He had entered the room from the front hallway where Ratch had helped him remove his mud-caked boots and breeches and the small stylus sticking from his hip.

"No, sir," said Ratch into the closet. "Merely your wife and stepson, entertaining."

" 'Merely'!" scoffed the marquis. " 'Merely my wife and stepson!' " He pushed his way farther back into the closet, struggling to pull shut the heavy paneled door behind him. "There is nothing the slightest bit 'mere' — nor 'entertaining,' now that you mention it — about anyone in that room and you know it! Now, let go at once, I command you!"

Ratch showed no sign of heeding his master's voice, though there are explanations as likely as brazen insubordination. It is possible that Ratch simply did not hear his lord's piteous entreaties from behind the ermines, minks and other sartorially sacrificed former woodland creatures into which Vadney was madly burrowing. (Had such creatures themselves had Vadney's instincts they might not have been hanging there in that coat closet in the first place.) It is also entirely possible that Vadney's pleas were never made audibly, at all, however he may have thought and intended to cry out. It has been observed and reported that in the presence of his nearest family, the marquis often behaved most peculiarly, losing one or more of his customary senses and/or faculties.

The point became moot when Ratch's heretofore unrelenting grip on the door's crystal knob gave way, suddenly. Vadney had stood as much chance of wresting the door from his servant's grip as he had of bare-handedly launching Nelson over the castle's battlements, but Ratch had ceased his share of the struggle. In other words, the marquis was an absolute lock to slam shut the door, had he not braced his foot in the frame for leverage. So forcefully did he slam said foot in the now-uncontested door that his scream was sure, he quailed at the thought, to disrupt his wife's earnest conference.

Amazingly, miraculously, mercifully, she paid this coat-closet conflict no evident attention, cradling (so much as her limited wingspan would allow) the strangely silent, Vadney half noticed, Nelson, and conversing with her companions.

Vadney made an escape, temporary he

knew all too well, that no limp could render un-celebratory.

    Lord Vadney lifted the glass to his pale lips and took a tentative sip. He swallowed with his eyes closed and nodded slightly.

    "Leave this bottle close by and bring another," he said.

    "Shall I bring some to her ladyship, my lord?"

    "Oh, god! Is she . . . ?" Lord Poon-Grebe scanned the room hastily, as if he might be snuck up upon and seized physically. He spied no such pressing danger and sank back into the brocaded wing-back chair. "No. Unless she calls for you directly you have my permission — and the survival sense, I suspect — to avoid her as a general rule."

"Yes, my lord."

"And, Ratch," said Lord Poon-Grebe to the exceedingly weary-looking servant.

"Yes, my lord?"

"Do try to avoid mention of me, even if called directly. I'd rather not be on her mind"

"Mum's the word, sir. But I believe that her ladyship may request you at some point tonight, sir."

"Did she say something, Ratch?" Lord Vadney's voice cracked ever so slightly.

"She alluded, sir. Yes."

"She alluded *me*, Ratch?" Or is it 'to me'? Alluded *to* me?"

"Sir . . ."

"What exactly did she say, Ratch?"

"Her ladyship, sir, upon seeing me descend to the wine cellar for this first bottle, said, I believe it was, sir, 'If that enfeebled sot cannot ascend of his own volition when I call, Ratch, I shall have you truss him and hoist him feet first, cracking his skull with each step.' "

Lord Vadney grimaced. "Yes, Ratch. You're right. She alluded me."

"Quite assertively, sir."

"Well, then," Lord Vadney puffed, rising from the chair. "Don't bother fetching that second bottle to me."

"No, sir."

Vadney grabbed his glass and the uncorked bottle.

"I'll be in the cellar if she beckons."

"Yes, sir. Shall I ready the ropes?"

Hours later, his lips now a vivid crimson, Lord Vadney stood in a vast stone room beneath Castle Grundel. Around the chamber were items of furniture with appearances as obscurely purposeful as they were clearly uncomfortable: long tables augmented with cogs and gears, festooned with leather straps or harnesses; cabinets or self-contained chambers scarcely large enough for a single occupant; low stools pitched and shaped so one could not balance an egg at the top, though one could display a glove or stocking. (How could one sit on such a stool? Perhaps best not to speculate.)

From thick beams at the joints of the overhead vaults hung buckled belts, chains linked to heavy wooden winches and other such mechanical paraphernalia, so the ceiling resembled the rigging of a mighty naval vessel.

Lord Vadney stood surveying the scene. This was not at all unusual: He often came to this wing of his cellar and gazed upon his devices. If one were to observe Lord Vadney contemplating these enigmatic engines, this ambiguous gear, one might (say, eight times out of ten) assume he had constructed them himself, for whatever vague and possibly unsettling purpose. (What was up with that stool?) His pride in this room shone from him enough to rival his habitual inebriate's flush.

But tonight was, statistically speaking, a ninth night. Tonight, Lord Vadney huffed and sighed. He paced around the room, eyeing its contents from many angles. He backed against a far wall, squinted and gazed down his extended arm over his upraised thumb. He squatted and craned his neck to peer at the taller accoutrements from a cat's vantage. He laid prone and stared at the weirdly webbed ceiling from a worm's-eye view. He groaned. He chewed the lace at his collar. Lord Vadney was vexed.

"Ratch, I am vexed."

Baggy-eyed Ratch, his nightshirt stuffed incompletely into his velvet breeches, did not immediately respond.

"You can see why I should be, can you not? This is all so bloody . . . so bloody . . ."

"Vexing, sir."

"Yes! Bloody vexing. Precisely."

Lord Vadney turned away from his man, missing Ratch's yawn, which was large enough to provide the illusion that the upper portion of his head was only loosely hinged to the lower.

But Ratch's exhausted exhalation, though impressive, was overmatched by

Lord Vadney's own: a great, long-suffering, mournful sigh full of sympathy for its own author.

"All right, then, Ratch. Let's keep at it. What if we moved the Judas Chair there, beside the Iron Maiden? That clears the floor space beneath the strappado and provides plenty of arm room for flagellation at the stocks. And it still leaves room and good flow, even with the addition of the Brazen Bull I've got my eye on. Though that might throw off the color scheme. Of course, I've been thinking of new tapestries for ages, anyway. Or is that too cozy for a dungeon, Ratch? It just gets so damp and chilly down here. It's good for the wine and the ambiance of dread but it's terrible for my sinuses."

As if on cue, Ratch sneezed tremendously.

The Jakes & Japes was, Cyril knew, a terrible tavern: The rooms were filthy, the furniture ramshackle, the fare so mysteriously flavored that among the patrons there existed a tacit compact to simply never guess. Additionally, the staff were arranged along a short personality spectrum from "rude" to "murderous" — with brief station stops at "deranged" and "contagious." There were in fact only three things to commend the Jakes & Japes to anyone: It was impossibly cheap; its drinks were toxically potent; and it had the only regular Amateur Recitation Night in the city. That might seem little enough, and far short of a recommendation, but for Cyril Shakewit these comprised a glorious trifecta. Because Cyril was habitually broke, profoundly thirsty and, not entirely coincidentally, a poet.

Now, the critical evaluation of poetry is a subtle and demanding practice requiring an education, a sensibility and a patience, none of which we possess. Furthermore, as even the most discerning academic will begrudgingly allow, *de gustibus non desputandum*, which translated roughly means "some people will swallow anything." So, in poetry, one man's "There Once Was a Knight From Gut Bucket" is another man's creation-myth allusion and subtly erotic water imagery. That being said, Cyril was an enormously unsuccessful poet. (In fact, the aforementioned "There Once Was a Knight from Gut Bucket," which was one of Cyril's early works, had gotten him thrashed badly and banned formally from the precinct of the city known as the Gut Bucket.)

Cyril wiped his greasy mouth on the

coarse-woven and frayed fabric of his sleeve, then downed half a tankard of the tavern's signature drink. It was only slightly rougher on his palate than his sleeve had been on his lips. "The Daisy" it was called. Many a red-faced, gasping newcomer to the J&J had retched at the seeming irony of that name. But no one who had known the drink's namesake, a former tap wench at the Jakes, was the least unprepared. And, in any event, those who had, as Cyril had, recently consumed the tavern's food were often fondly disposed to the Daisy's exfoliating properties on both mouth and memory.

"Succulent!" Cyril cried out.

"Suck your what?!"

Cyril ducked beneath the long wooden bench on which he'd wolfed down his meal, explaining hastily, "No, love! Easy! It means 'rich, delicious, scrumptious, delectable, a wonderment and whirlwind of the culinary craft, a great gift granted by the gustatory gods and goddesses."

The patter had slowed the menacing advance of the serving girl, rumored to be, Cyril knew, a not-too-distant relative of the legendary Daisy, but it had not softened her gaze.

"Bloody good grub, Dolly! Did I detect a soupçon, the faintest hint of . . ."

"Shut it!" The protest of other diners not so many tankards into the night as Cyril and, as such, still susceptible to reckless speculation re: ingredients quieted him. But his plain-spoken appeal had seemingly satisfied the waitress that her honor had not been slighted — or not in any intriguing manner, anyway. She'd returned to her deliveries of drafts and dreck. Cyril grabbed the still-half-full tankard, jovially patted the shoulder of a dining companion (a tiny man with an outrageous and assertive mustache, clasping a fistful of paper money the strange source of which he had boasted of to Cyril in an anecdote Cyril was unable to follow in the slightest) and left the main dining area for the back of the tavern where the city's unknown bards, balladeers, jugglers, jesters, stage mages and freelance idiots were already gathering to sign up for their slots on the evening's bill.

Once a week every week since its founding the tavern had invited performers of any type to tread the boards, as it were (really, just rough planks set across some upturned apple crates) in the Jakes's back room. The most popular performer of the evening, usually discernible from the lesser by an absence of vegetable matter clinging to his or her person had their night's tab covered by the house. This created an interesting dynamic of artistic ambition and competitive opportunism.

As there was no time limit for the night's entertainment, the winner would often be announced quite late. Few performers wanted to stint on their ability to rack up a hefty bill of which to absolved. The confident and logical thing to do, then, was to gulp and guzzle with at least as much focus as one thought to perform. This was surely the best tactic for the truly talented. There were, though, complications to this strategy: 1) All performers were also audience members, so the deck was stacked rather against anyone with evident talent simply due to the fact that the viewers quite hoped everyone they observed would fail spectacularly and would not scruple to help them do so in whatever way they could drunkenly conjure; 2) the earlier mentioned quality of the Jakes & Japes fare and the heavy drinking that accompanied it had both an accelerating effect on the competitiveness and an inhibitive — really, more a narcotic — effect on any natural talent brought to bear. It was perhaps the tavern's one truly inspired recipe: For every one winner there were dozens of stuffed, drunk, full-fare paying losers.

Part talent show, part drinking competition, part con, part bloodsport, the Jakes & Japes Amateur Recitation Night was known throughout the city of Boyledin, from the lowliest guttersnipe to the highest-born courtier.

Opinions on the event varied from zealous dedication to furious approbation; but evinced no predictable pattern *vis a vis* the social standing of the bearer: Ragged street preachers and the most elevated ecclesiastical officials decried the rude spectacle from their respective ad hoc and privileged podiums; politicians from the meanest, most corrupt borough warden to the most decorated and corrupt court counsel promised to rout this pernicious blemish on the fair girlish face of public morality and decorum. While at the same time, prostitutes and parliamentarians, both, ceased their trickery long enough catch at least a portion of the evening's entertainments; and any given gathering was likely to have near-equal number of nefarious and the noble. This democratic representation was not confined, surprisingly enough, to the ranks of onlookers. While the bulk of the evening's aspirants were hoi-polloi, it was known that the quality — though perhaps an off-brand or irregular type thereof — had distinguished themselves with notable turns. A certain duke, now little seen in town, was commonly believed to owe his habit of never doffing his kid gloves or skull cap and never sitting in public to an "earthy" and crowd-pleasing fire-juggling routine some decades before.

    Legion were the legendary performances of Amateur Recitation Night's gone by: Garrick Purejoy's Miraculous Obedient Wharf Rats made their debut at the Jakes; as did Lady Arabella, the Licentious Levitationist. "The Ballad of the Big-Balled Barber" was first performed there, reportedly, though its original orator is much in dispute, with as many claiming credit as renouncing utterly. That infamous troupe of rogue Maurice Dancers, the

Maurice Sons, long banished to the Continent and recently rumored to have perished in a single bathtub, had their first run in with the constabulary during Amateur Recitation Night; and Geoffrey Renard, himself, whose "You Might Be a Jackanapes" has driven the crowned heads of this hemisphere half mad with hilarity, began his performing career at the Jakes. The Jakes & Japes was a motley of high and low, of refined and rotten, of glittering and greasy, paupers drunk as lords and lords drunk as even-drunker lords.

 Cyril Shakewit felt comfortable here as he did no other place. Here, society seemed more porous, more permeable than elsewhere. It seemed riddled with passageways, a hub, a transfer station trading tickets for talent — or novelty or oddity or audacity as the collective mood might have it. Cyril liked to think of himself as talented (he was not, particularly) and he flattered himself to think he would never suffer the condescension of those who awarded fleeting fame to mere freaks, but in his heart of hearts . . . . Well, won't most of us take what we can get? Don't we all have a trace of lace-collared dog-faced boy in us?

But Cyril was an optimist of marked fortitude. He had believed himself destined for great things for as long as he could remember; and though great things had thus far seemed wholly unaware and unmoved by Cyril's belief, he was not swayed. In fact, Fortune's lackadaisical attitude toward Cyril's inevitable elevation only convinced him that he should have to force the issue. And where better than the Jakes and when better than tonight?

Lady Camilla Fitz-Victim Poon-Grebe was a striking figure. It was not uncommon at all for one to feel struck by her. This was remarked upon even by those who had not been struck by her. She was somehow both avian and geometric, as if someone had worked hard to build a bird of prey out of nothing but straight lines, flat planes and hard angles. There was no hint of those things that roughly symbolized the place in the food chain of other fowl: the plumage, the plumpness here or there. Lady Poon-Grebe instead looked like murder expressed mathematically, the square root of a raptor.

Whatever softness the Fitz blood would allow — Camilla's very corpuscles must have been square — had manifested itself in her son, Nelson, an ovoid. It is possible that Nelson's precociously bloated figure came from his biological father, Lady Camilla's previous husband, Lord Osgood Victim. Some recall a youthful reputation for joyful hijinks and indulgence in that man before marriage. It is even rumored that the preposterously wealthy young noble was purposely wed to his austere bride by parents fearful that his prodigious appetites would prove the better of even their staggering accumulation of lucre. Be that as it may, for all the speculation and nostalgia and gossip, no reliable recollection of Lord Victim before his demise remains save that of a gaunt, almost spectral, figure in a night dress draped on his frame like a white flag on a windless day.

 Under Camilla's care, Lord Victim's legacy, both filial and financial, flourished to, some might say, shocking — even obscene — dimensions. It was these that she brought to the marriage to Lord Vadney

Poon-Grebe, who in turn provided little liquidity but enormous land holdings and, it goes almost without saying, the venerable Poon-Grebe name. (As if we needed to explain that! Who in all of Maybia is unfamiliar with the Poon-Grebes significance to this great empire?) And if the union, in the eyes of some cynical, politically minded commentators was transparently opportunistic it was in no way a settled matter who was getting the better of whom.

It was, in fact, an open secret, that neither party in this marriage of convenience did without, really, rather a great deal of inconvenience. The fact was, for her part, Camilla loathed her current husband, thoroughly. That, loathing thoroughly, was one of the things at which she excelled. Money management and white-hot hatred were perhaps her most particular gifts. Those two, and the somewhat disharmonious note of maternal devotion: For Lady Camilla Fitz-Victim Poon-Grebe loved her fat little Nelson as much as she loved money and, more impressively, quite as much as she disapproved of nearly everybody else.

As for Nelson, himself . . . well. It is difficult to comment upon Nelson in details other than the shallow and strictly physical. This is not due solely to the boy's remarkable girth, though allow us for a moment to comment upon it, Nelson's remarkable girth:

Nelson was fat in the manner that stars are stand-offish; in the fashion that the ocean has mood swings; in the way that gravity is grabby. Nelson was not pudgy, nor stocky, nor husky. One could not picture Nelson growing to be lumbering, bear-like or even massive. Nelson could only grow, one had to think, to be fat -er. He was all the qualities of fat: He was soft, yielding and unfirm. (He was his mother's anti-being, and the philosophers and astrologers of the day may well have been tempted toward assaying a weighty, so to speak, tome on the significance of the boy's birth, were they not so terrified of the maternal critique of such a work.)

If it seems unkind to perseverate on young Nelson's physique, let us say in our defense that there was little else upon which to hang descriptors. Even if the boy's size had been this side of outlandish, one would be hard pressed to distinguish him. He was occasionally quite loud, there was that. When it suited him, Nelson could howl a gale. In pleasure, pain or pique, Nelson was amplified. Nelson was volume.

But these obvious attributes aside, Nelson displayed little that one could comfortably term a personality. If he spoke, few could say. He was never seen publicly but in the care and company of his mother, who consistently spoke for him. One presumes that one of Lady Camilla's servants must have had some interaction of substance with the boy, but they all seemed to have been selected to service for their temperamental resemblance to their mistress. It was better, therefore, not to inquire. Lord Vadney and Ratch, if only by proximity, must have some insight and privileged perspective. But to question either about Nelson brought such a haunted, hunted look to their eyes (even staunch Ratch!) that it seemed cruel to press.

    Nelson Poon-Grebe was a creature of

curiosity and slightly awed confusion, like a basilisk, a pygmy or a giraffe. He was viewed askance, overheard cringingly, and was perhaps not known truly to anyone, at all.

The point is that Nelson, while inarguably a minor evil in and around Castle Grundel, was not very much paid attention to at a conscious level. He had become like a kind of native nettle, an indigenous irritant. Fat, terrible, tantrumy Nelson was just a fact of lice, er, life.

So, it was a kind of semi-conscious relief — as when it occurs to one that winter has given way to spring and the sun has decided to hang around a bit longer and, why, has been showing up quite a bit, recently, hasn't he? Isn't great to have the old boy back? — when word spread that something was the matter with young Nelson.

Now of course, none of the castle residents or the townspeople wished the boy any positive harm. They were not so callous. He was however rotten a boy, still just a boy. But they could hardly be blamed for enjoying the hiatus. For Nelson had gone still.

The rest of Castle Grundel was, predictably, in an uproar.

Cyril was involved in an intense negotiation. Or, rather, more accurately, Cyril was intensely involved in a negotiation. Or, even more accurately, Cyril was intensely involved in trying to convince an utterly implacable Dolly to subtract from his bill the cost of the produce he had cleaned from his garments and hair.

"Dolly, look at this! This isn't even a side salad! It's a meal, in itself!" Cyril was pitching hard. "What is this? Why, I think this is a tomato — at this time of year? Who would even throw this? And I'm not even looking to make profit. Just subtract it from the bill. That's a great deal for the house."

Dolly's expression was the exact opposite of mysterious.

"Doll, look here. What would you say to a little escarole?"

Dolly's right hand, the one still holding

the heavy, solid wood trencher, shot out Cyril-ward. "I warned you about that filthy talk," she said coldly, as Cyril, from his back, counted out coins. The night was not going at all as he had hoped.

Amazingly, the crowd had not responded favorably to what Cyril had thought a tight and sure-fire set. He'd opened with a parodic sonnet about the loveliness of this particular crowd, one he'd honed to the very razor's edge between ingratiating and backhanded; he'd sidled smoothly into a lightly political, slightly saucy rhyme about poaching royal deer and then got going full steam with a galloping terza rima about the military ineptness and libidinal liberties of a pair of country lads conscripted into service in the recent fracas in the Straits of Bazooka. Cyril himself greatly admired the bit for its structural complexity and ribald energy (one specific syphilis joke, particularly), though he feared secretly that some of the rhymes were forced.

"Ugh. Terza rima," he groaned, propping himself up on his elbows.

"Is that what you were drinking? What, is that a brand name of turpentine?" A hand extended to Cyril to help him to his feet.

"Thanks, friend. No, terza rima . . ."

"Was never going to fly with this crowd, though it was ambitious of you to try. But this is, I believe, more a 'moon-June' audience. I fear that 'wine-dark sea and buggery' were perhaps a bit too . . . classical."

"That rhyme scheme is a nightmare. I don't know what I was thinking," Cyril said with self-contempt.
His new companion responded comfortingly, "I thought it was quite daring.

You should be proud."

"Really? Well, that's decent of you to say."

"In your closing bit, the limerick . . ."

"Oh, I'd gotten desperate by that point."

"Yes, well, I expect the cabbages had some effect."

"Some of them were frozen solid, you know."

"I suspected. They made a frightful noise."

"The boys in Bazooka could use those. If I can come up with something to rhyme with 'cabbages' I might try to work it in. Might be a kind of patriotic crowd pleaser."

"I don't know that crowd pleasing is the way for you, if you pardon the presumption."

"No?"

"Well, as I was saying, your limerick

reminded me a bit of the early work of Errol the Irregular."

Cyril, having been so recently on the floor of the Jakes & Japes and, therefore highly motivated never to return, would otherwise have been floored.

"You know the work of Errol the Irregular?!"

"Oh, of course. He was a groundbreaker. I thought your formal inclusiveness might be a nod to him. I mean, terza rima and limerick in one set . . . "

The men said in unison "The Rambunctious Tour of aught eight."

"Who are you?" Cyril cried. "I've never met anyone in this area who knows Errol the Irregular so well."

"It is a sad fact that few appreciate Errol's sublime craft. His passing was tragic and premature — or prompt, depending on your view. My name is Ratch, sir. I'm the Marquis D'Isle D'Eaux's man, at the Castle Grundel."

"Oh, sure. Poon-Grebe. He's quite a character, I hear."

"He is, in his own way, not unlike you, an ambitious and artistic man."

"But that wife of his. Sheesh."

"Best not speak of it, sir. People may still be eating."

"Good point. Probably mum on that preposterous child of theirs, as well."

"Well," Ratch's eyes shifted about.

"Can I ask you what you're doing at the Jakes, Ratch? Rumor has it that your master has, no offense, peculiar tastes, but I didn't think they ran quite this rough. And it would be too flattering to consider that you were here to see me."

"No."

Cyril tried to look nonchalant, as his face slid a barely perceptible fraction of a measurement down his face.

"I am," Ratch said nodding toward a crowded and boisterous table, "here, I'm sorry to say, for her."

"You're here for . . ." Cyril's face now puddled stylishly in a ruff around his neck.

"Yes," Ratch said, his voice edging toward complaint. "For tonight's winner."

Lord and Lady Poon-Grebe met in the west drawing room, for which Vadney secretly thanked the wise Ratch with nearly the force he had blasphemed when the man had delivered Camilla's peremptory summons. The room was the only in which Vadney felt safe with his wife: It was enormous, and littered with divans, busts on pedestals and other obstacles. Its paneled walls contained many means of egress, which Vadney knew as well as he knew the backs of his moderately trembling hands.

"Whatever you think best, of course, my dear," he said in his manliest placating tone. "It's just that I'm not sure I follow your thoughts on Nelson's . . . on his . . . his condition."

"No. I'm quite sure you don't," his wife responded in, really, the only tone one can imagine such a response. (It should be noted, perhaps, the Lady Camilla had rather few tones in her kit from which to choose.)

"But shouldn't we ask the advice of Dr. Swann?"

"That quack?!"

Lord Vadney knew this would be delicate moment at which to laugh. In the euphemistic best of times his wife distrusted levity. At this moment frivolity could prove suicidal. Instead, he coughed into his sleeve.

"Well, yes. Or rather, no. He has an absolutely sterling reputation, you know."

"A reputation for acquiring sterling, I'm sure." Lady Camilla was not to be moved on the local physician, it was obvious.

"Another, then. If we're sending to the city, why not for a proper doctor?"

"Because, Vadney, you clot, his condition, as you so timidly put it, is well beyond the ken or care of a money-grubbing sawbones. My dear sweet boy, my darling Nelson, the poor, poor lamb."

Lord Vadney coughed into his other sleeve.

" My dear poor child is having a spiritual crisis. He is beset by forces that wish to taint his child's pure heart. Dark currents that could carry away his very loving, blessed soul!"

"Yes, dear, so you said. I think it's there you lost me. Y'see . . . "

Lady Camilla's voice was never pleasing. But her next utterance could have given a brick a nervous tremor: "Nelson is possessed."

Though not generally a superstitious man, Lady Camilla's arcane contention was one of the least difficult to believe Vadney had ever heard.

"What, because of the screaming and

such? I suppose that would explain it. But I thought you said it was to do with bile, or something. Showed leadership qualities. I agree possession makes more sense, but in any event, he's been really quite quiet recently, now that we're speaking of it. Bit of a relief, really."

Somewhere a brick borrowed nails to bite.

"That is exactly what I'm talking about, you brain-boiled goat! He has been utterly silent and still for two days and a night! Some infernal minion has been dispatched to rob us of our brightest, most vital light forever! There is a battle, a battle for the soul of our — of my — son to be joined!"

"Is he not just sleepy?"

It was fortunate for Lord Vadney that he had long ago developed the habit of keeping some item of furniture or lesser-prepared servant or houseguest between himself and Lady Camilla whenever possible. It was a shame about the tea cup and he had no idea if bone china could easily be removed from a taxidermy mink but, a narrow escape is an escape, still.

The heavy oak paneled door could not quite block out the shrill caw, "Possessed!"

The crowd around the largest table in the Jakes's dining room was packed as densely as the grounds at any coronation or execution, the moods as varied. The winner of the Amateur Recitation Night sat there attracting well wishers, glad handers, and on hangers. The usual drink filchers and pocket pickers worked the less tightly compacted margins. But in addition to the adoring and the opportunistic, there were the indignant and the outraged.

Among the latter ranks were, of course, the sore losers. But while such provide entertainment, we are not concerned with them. Instead, we are interested in those assembled — both performers and patrons — who suspected, believed deeply or were howling like blood-drunk cannibals that a fundamental precept, a foundational principle, a central and defining part of the hallowed Jakes & Japes Amateur Recitation Night tradition had been violated by the very person this same assembly had pronounced the victor.

For, the most recent champion, seated calmly, entirely unperturbed in the midst of the tavern tumult, had eaten and drunk that night — not one thing. The entire amount that this popular hero would be forgiven, the sum total of this particular absolution, the full yield of this jubilee moment, the precise figure to the furthest point reckoned that would be erased, expunged, blotted from the ledger of the venerable Jakes & Japes Tavern this night and forever more was not one paltry coin.

The collective mind of the crowd reeled, which, added to the preexisting Daisy-induced reeling, produced a cumulative reel sufficient to generate a magnetic field permanently skewing by five degrees the onboard compasses of two sailing ships docked nearby. Months later, this would result in the loss of 75 nautical souls and the discovery of a lost continent of shockingly vulgar but otherwise highly evolved flightless birds. But that is a tale for another volume.

To have entered the J&J Amateur Recitation Night, to have sat waiting for one's introduction while all around you wolfed eel pies, porridge, roasts, whole buckets of potatoes, vats of mutton stew and enough alcohol to bewilder many advanced nations and to cripple, blind and sterilize any in its idyllic aboriginal state, to do so without so much as a glass of cool water . . .

When it was revealed that the winner had, in fact, literally, refused a glass of cool water the Night Watch was called in to restore order.

The outcry resulting from this unprecedented deviation was a psychologically complex phenomenon. As mentioned, there were the run-of-the-mill sore losers. But we must tear ourselves away from them. Much as we, professionally, have interest in the petty and the vengeful (for where would the storytellers be without grudges?), those are not our subjects. There were also those who felt duped and threatened - the proprietors of the Jakes among those most unnerved. Talented teetotalers or ascetics upset the entire appetitive ecosystem and economics of Amateur Recitation Night. There were those, too, who took affront at the face-value flouting of tradition: The simple feared change simply, the more sophisticated and conservative believed tradition a bulwark against anarchy. And there were some, a not insignificant percentage, who just found this night's triumphant contestant . . . weird.

Lord Vadney Poon-Grebe, 13th Marquis D'Isle D'Eaux, strolled the portrait gallery leading to his library. Shallow alcoves scalloped the marble wall, each housing imperious paintings of Vadney's accomplished forebears: starting with the very first marquis, the near-mythological warrior Leslie Evelyn Aubrey Poon-Grebe, a man whose natural belligerence would have earned him the scaffold in times of peace, or even modern war. But Vadney's many-times great grandfather had been fortunate to have been born in an era when his ferocity could be regarded as a national resource rather than, as it would surely have been in later generations, a worrisome symptom or a civic menace. It was from Leslie that the Poon-Grebe's eminence derived.

Unsure borders and a nervous king (at

that time, little more than that battle season's luckiest warlord) bought Leslie a large parcel of land, highly desirable but for its placement on the ever-twitching boundary between homeland and the westernmost province of the enormous, near-Continent-consuming B'zerki Empire. King Waxwroth had gifted Leslie this lush and fertile march on the Isle d'Eaux, positioned between a small river and the channel known as the Gwylf (translated from the local dialect: "water bigger'n that one there but not so big as that great big one over there that we was talkin' about afore"). The bequest was a reward for Leslie's military service in the struggles among competing nobles at home. Home being, at that time, a loose and unstable affiliation of feudal landlords still animated by the suspicions and animosities of their own tribal ancestors. By dint of being a shade less dim, a shade more ambitious or just by cutting the most striking profile on the recently centralized coinage, Waxwroth had managed to beat these nobles into the shape of a kingdom, more or less.

The "less" being concentrated almost exclusively on his eastern border. In fact, the B'Zerki still held half the island in question. But by rewarding his most competent (read: maniacally homicidal) fighting man with a permanent post and a vested interest on his most vulnerable ground, Waxwroth hoped to serve multiple goals: Firstly and obviously, to secure the east against the B'zerki; secondly, to be seen as a munificent regent who amply rewarded loyalty in the face of danger and stiff opposition, and thirdly and passionately, to rid himself of regular personal contact with

Lord Leslie Evelyn Aubrey Poon-Grebe, who was flat-out terrifying, when it came down to it.

The stratagem was successful beyond expectation. Not only did Lord Leslie chase the B'zerki off the land granted him, the western portion of the Isle d'Eaux, but out of the eastern portion, as well. And then across the channel, hereafter known as the Poon, and many leagues across the Continent. Lord Leslie was suddenly the largest landholder in the newly unified, freshly expanded and nearly foe-less nation, which Waxwroth, master of purposeful and self-serving gift, named Maybia, after his temperamental wife. Lord Leslie's marquisate was something slightly faster than immediate in its bestowal.

Gazing upon the heroic portrait, the very brushstrokes of which were rudely potent,

Lord Vadney slumped. He kept his eyes down as he shuffled past the next ten of his predecessors, each distinguished in his own right, each larger than life. He paused at the 12th Marquis d'Isle d'Eaux and gathered himself up to face his father, Lord Hilary Clare Bristol Poon-Grebe. Prepared. Got ready.

Getting ready.

Just about ready.

Nope.

In the library, Vadney threw himself on a lounge he had placed optimally for that function. It faced large glass-paned doors that opened onto a balcony, which on exceptionally clear days gave view to the distant Poon. Fortunately the damp climate and frequent rains prevented that sight from occurring more than Vadney could bear. Instead, he gazed more usually upon the rain framed in the dark wood of the doors and the busts on the pedestals that flanked them. These were heroes he could handle.

Two on the left: Gaius Epiglottis Voracious, the only member of the classical Palomian Legislature ever put to death for corrupting the morals of, quote, "just, well, pretty much everyone, really;" and Count Radu Zamfir, the Black Saint of the White Mountain (or Necre Svent per Albamonte, for native speakers of Vladistanian). Two on the right: "Gorgeous" George Lord Barron, the adventurer and pornographic poet; and, of course, Vadney's personal idol, Sir Nigel St. Rapeen, the prolific memoirist and pervert. (Or, more accurately, memoirist and prolific pervert; for, voluminous as it was, Sir Nigel's lengthy and detailed chronicle did not constitute but rather described his most astonishing output.

Input. Both, really, alternately.)

These men were artists. They were refined, sublime in their sensitivities. Men of such discernment, taste and experience that they were not mere passive props or pawns of their respective times. They were crafters of unique, personalized, tailored cultures — they were self-contained cultures. Did they transgress? Oh, indeed, they did! With idiosyncratic élan hardly matched by the most bellicose generals of history, who — let's call a mace a mace — were really just muddy, truculent civil servants, anyway. There's a man behind the man behind the man behind the infantry; and it's usually just some sort of fancy-dress clerk with a uni degree and the ear of the king. Yes, even Vadney's own most-martial ancestors took orders, it was likely, from some posh twit from St. Juicy's College, some inky git schooled in rhetoric, logic and sodomy.

    Vadney caught himself yelling this last aloud. He thought it might be best to pour himself a drink. He was fraught with anxiety tonight. He usually found himself in a kind of quiet, semi-erotic reverie throughout his stays at the Castle Grundel, but Nelson's condition ("possession," he huffed to no one) and the consequent forced interaction with his wife was ruining everything. Bad enough to return from his anticlimactic amble around the countryside to be greeted with his family, but by those terrible friends of hers, as well: Lady Mantiss was a kind of walking temperance lecture and Lady Sauvignon — well, if Vadney were to be honest, Lady Sauvignon's sultry airs mystified and intimidated him, wildly. She'd married a Puissian, after all! No doubt she'd had some influence in his wife's outlandish diagnosis.

Vadney poured himself another brimming crystal globe of Flenish Elk Marrow brandy. Flenish Elk Marrow Brandy is not named, as one might logically conclude, due to any Northlander knack for distilling deer tissue, but a common colloquial Flenish phrase describing the effects of this tipple: "hoof prints in your blood."

"This whole thing is daft," Vadney thought. "Loony. So the boy's quiet. Isn't it about bloody time? It had to be coming eventually, hadn't it? That's just the Law of, whatzit, Something or Other. The, uh . . . Oh! Newton Isaacson's First Law of Commotion! That's it: 'An objectionable commotion stays a commotion until you're unbalanced, or it needs a rest.' That sounds right. Nelson just needs a bit of a rest."

He poured himself another drink, feeling rather proud of himself for his scholarly acumen. "Pthhhpppt on St. Juicy's, anyway," he said to himself. "College, schmollege. Bunch of noodles in their ivory gowns and their silk towers. Bah. Inkpots. Quill jockeys. Secretaries!"

Perhaps it was a reaction to his earlier rumination on the nature of heroism; perhaps it was his thoughts on the man of true independent spirit and the freedom of expression; perhaps it was a hemoglobic herd of arctic ungulates running roughshod in his circulatory system, but Vadney thought it was an ideal moment to revisit the subject of Nelson with Lady Camilla. The whinnying blood elk concurred.

Mistress Ekaterina Blatatat sat in the middle of a bench at the longest table in the

Jakes & Japes. She was flanked and faced by people yelling themselves hoarse contending this or that fine point of her win at the Amateur Recitation Night. The argument had complicated currents: Participants found themselves arguing one way, only to find another shouting partisan with the same opinion and suddenly taking the opposite stance in an automatic accommodation of the prevailing antagonism. Before too long one would argue one's way around to one's original point of view to find oneself engaged in heated debate with oneself, beating oneself into complete agreement with oneself, and feeling pleased to have finally found both a worthy foe and reasonable ally.

The ranks of debaters were a half-dozen deep. Mistress Blatatat was completely surrounded by combatants making a kind of human coliseum around her. For all the violent expression, she was calm and unaffected, for all anyone could tell.

She wore a simple high- and stiff-necked dress lacking in adornment. Her hair was pulled in a bun on the top of her head. Her attire was not exactly austere, but it was in most ways designed to repel attention. She did nothing to accentuate any one aspect of her physical self over another. (A rather stunning lack of vanity. For who among us does not betray our secret pride in this or that personal trait? With luxurious lotions for unblemished skin, spectacles of rare materials to frame a fine face, expensive pomades for imposing mustaches, or lengthy humorous compositions delivered regularly to the sternly judgmental publishing houses of our city?)

If Mistress Blatatat projected any one

identifiable personal attribute, it was patience. She waited to be apprehended holistically. She did not need to distort or exaggerate. She was supremely self-possessed. Mistress Blatatat did not trouble herself with the hubbub surrounding her, at all. She could have been seated in a a comfortable parlor listening to the latest composition for bowl organ by the virtuosic Wilberforce Cluck, rather than to the full-throated howls of Daisy-reeking tavern contestants cheated, they thought, out of a dipsomaniacal windfall.

After a time the most vociferous grew raspy and winded, allowing for the manager of the Jakes, an undersized man named Bevis Thrunt to make himself heard. Thrunt was in a curious position: While the "house" keeps odds long, it knows that payouts must be frequent and reliable enough to maintain the illusion that a sucker can get an even break. Mistress Blatatat was in violation of an unspoken compact. She was upsetting the applecart. Thrunt was shrewd enough to perceive this only dimly, but he was certainly quick enough to grasp that the shadowy owner of the tavern did not like trouble, did not like change and, if rumors are to be believed, valued no human soul nor any number of such over even the smallest denomination of Maybian currency (the ha'flake, if you are a foreigner).

"Mistress Blatatat, if I could? You know, of course, that the Jakes & Japes Amateur Recitation Night has a long history."

Mistress Blatatat looked at Thrunt impassively, betraying no nameable emotion. Thrunt hesitated briefly, as if he'd hoped that slight statement would have sufficed.

"In that history, never once has the establishment failed or hesitated to deliver on its promise of reward. This reputation is quite important to us."

Mistress Blatatat spoke softly but very clearly. "Your reputation should not suffer. You promise to excuse the debt incurred by consumption. All I have consumed while here tonight is air and attention. I believe your traditional charge for such is nothing. You have recompensed me fully, then."

Thrunt spoke with a slight strain. To anyone else, to everyone else, it was clear that Thrunt, while in no way physically impressive, was nervous enough to be unpredictable and dangerous. He had the look of a man who slept with a weapon and a list of ready alibis.

"Hm. Yes. But, Mistress Blatatat, our reputation is really rather more, uh, specific that that. Which is to say, our reputation is not for excusing bills in the abstract but in a more, well, a markedly more alcoholic fashion. And is important to our clientele, as you can tell, in precisely that same way."

Mistress Blatatat was quietly adamant. "I cannot myself consume your spirits or your fare. I'm sorry but that is impossible. But I can help you honor your tradition and maintain the trust of your patrons, I believe."

Thrunt's mustache twitched hopefully.

"Who is possession of the largest unsettled bill with this tavern?" Mistress Blatatat pitched her voice more for the assembled crowed than for Thrunt, but Thrunt paid no heed and answered straight away.

"The grandest individual total accrued tonight," he pronounced, consulting a handy ledger, "is that of Ivor of Roday, who owes 60 royal yelps."

Now, 60 royal yelps spent on food and drink by a single Maybian is a staggering amount — more than a month's pay for even a townsperson with a valued trade like Leech Wrangler, Filthwife or Midden Keep. But Mistress Blatatat pressed.

"No, not the largest total tonight. The largest outstanding sum — ever."

The crowd as one turned silently toward Thrunt, who stood gape-mouthed, limp-mustached, ledger open, then to the opposite end of the room closest to the bar. There, atop a cask, propped against a wall, near hidden from sight slumped a man in rough-spun, stained clothes.

Someone whispered: "Guzzle." It was said in a tone that echoed of awe and majesty and reverence, of canyons or cathedrals.

Mistress Blatatat said simply, "Yes, then him."

Thrunt stuttered, "H-him? Him, what?"

"I grant my prize to Guzzle."

Thrunt blinked hard, then flipped hurriedly through his ledger to back pages edged in red. He ran his finger down first one column, then another, then another — then turned the page. His eyes widened as his lips moved, counting silently. Or perhaps praying.

The others in the dining room were talking among themselves. One word was more frequent than any other. It bubbled through the susurration and grew louder. It took shape and rhythm. It became a chant.

"Guz.Zle. Guz.Zle. Guz.ZLE. GUZ.ZLE!" went the call.

"Nooooooooo.Nononnonononnooooooo

o," went Thrunt.

He waved his arms wildly, hitting no fewer than three people solidly in the heads with the heavy ledger.

"Mistress, the forgiveness, the prize . . . "

"Which I won."

" . . . is for performance . . ."

"Which I presented."

" . . . and for fare consumed in the course of that same night!"

"During which and of which I did not partake."

"Well, yes, quite so!" Thrunt's mustache gleamed. "But he is not the winner!"

"Then I renounce the prize and you are not out a single ha'flake."

"GUZ.ZLE! GUZ.ZLE! GUZ.ZLE!"

"He owes in excess of 33,000 royal yelps!"

"GUZ.ZLE! GUZ.ZLE! GUZ.ZLE!"

"He has been unconscious for 11 days!"

"GUZ.ZLE! GUZ.ZLE! GUZ.ZLE!"

"He drank all the Cracked Abbey Ale and most of the lamp fuel!"

"GUZ.ZLE! GUZ.ZLE! GUZ.ZLE!"

"He ate seven whole ducks, a lamb, three candles and half a lodging-room curtain!"

Thrunt's pleas were drowned out by the chanting and his resolve by Mistress Blatatat's glacial calm. He desisted, and after moments, so, too did Guzzle's fan club.

Thrunt looked around the room desperately, then made a gesture as if to simultaneously surrender and ward off evil. He tore three red-limned page from the ledger and the Jakes's patrons cheered and grew raucous afresh.

"You have made a decision that will please your employer, if he is a wise man, and I think he is," said Mistress Blatatat, almost kindly. "He is, after all, as you've indicated, wise enough to know that reputation is currency, too."

Lord Vadney stood his ground as capably as he could, given the ground's current rambunctious non-cooperation.

"Damn it, Camilla, the boy's just got the mung or the ague or something. It's a far leap to bloody possession. It's more likely the exhaustion of a short lifetime of shrieking."

"Don't you pollute the air in my proximity with your coarse vernacular; and don't you presume to know Nelson better than I. I have little confidence that you'd be able to pick Nelson from a crowd of boys, much less can you render a sound diagnosis."

"A crowd of boys? A crowd of boys?!"

Vadney windmilled his arms first for emphasis then for balance. "What I would give to see Nelson in a crowd of boys! Running, frolicking, torturing small amphibians, and the like. Proper boy activities! Nelson's never had a male friend — a friend! — in his life. If I didn't know better, I'd attribute his recent lassitude to ladies' ailments!"

"Vadney! How dare you be so vulgar and flippant?"

But Vadney was barreling ahead: "And find him? In the largest crowd of boys, in a battalion of identical boys, in a dragoon of doppelgängers, a county of copies, in a bloody nation of Nelsons I would find him with the greatest alacrity by first merely finding your apron and following the bloody strings!"

"Are you quite done?" asked Lady

Camilla in a tone against which Vadney's BEC (blood-elk content) was insufficient insulation. The brief euphoria, the pleasant weightlessness Vadney had felt during his minor rant, as if he had at long last loosed the ballast, was gone. He felt empty and slight.

"Yes. I suppose so."

"Sit down." The statement permitted no negotiation but that was beside the point, as Vadney very much wanted to sit down.

"Nelson is very clearly under the sway of some nefarious influence. Living here, he has of course been exposed to the example and potential influence of debased and vitiated nobility. I have however strived to protect him from the specifics of your pernicious perverse inclinations, your spiritual weakness and moral laxity. I dare say I have had some success. As you point out — yes, I understand that you intend such observation as chastisement and complaint — Nelson has had the fortitude and character to withstand any temptation toward, as you so roughly refer to such endeavors, frolicking. Eleven years, Vadney. In eleven years, Nelson has never once directed his natural vigor toward any but the most laudable directions: home and family. I know by motherly instinct, long observation and ample evidence that no tawdry, worldly lure could tap and siphon my Nelson so. Not even your own — his adoptive father's! — lurid example of a wastrel's ways could nudge Nelson in the least toward indulgence or ethical torpor. He has been waylaid, it is clear, by a supernatural agent bent on sapping the good and the pure strength that is our one terrestrial defense against the myriad devilments that weaker, cracked and ill-made souls, such as yourself, fall prey to, like field mice to weasels."

Vadney looked at her, agog. It had many years since he and his wife had so many words (or he had so many from her, as was really currently the case). He had almost forgotten what a stunning effect it could have. If he were in any condition to speak eloquently and had been asked to describe the experience of enduring his wife's oration, he would have said, "a bit like being put through a grist mill with a hymnal, without the satisfaction of thinking the hymnal was getting its comeuppance, too."

But Vadney said no such thing, as he was in no such shape. Instead, he said, "But, what . . . ?"

Lady Camilla raised an admonitory finger, and Vadney abandoned his search for the rest of his sentence.

"The effect of remaining so resolute has cost poor Nelson, dearly. Could you not see the struggle he underwent? Could you not hear his piteous cries? He has fallen into a spiritual slumber, exhausted and silenced by his fight to be good and pure despite the wickedness and the weakness around him. He has, as a last defense, retreated within."

Vadney mustered up the clarity to ask, "Could we not just send him to, say, Purel-on-the-Sea," invoking the name of the most celebrated sanitarium and spa in Maybia.

"Oh, you may be assured that he will be taken immediately to a more suitable environment. I have already been in communication with the headmaster of the Sebastian Academy for Curious Boys. If Nelson can be safely raised and restored to his former self, neither he nor I shall continue to suffer the poisonous effect of your libertine's extravagances."

Vadney stared at Camilla. He said nothing. Outwardly, he showed no sign of having heard or processed a thing she had uttered. So long was Vadney's blank pose that, had Camilla believed in his soul, she might have thought that it, too, was a battleground of light and dark forces. (But of course she did not.)

Only seconds before Camilla gave way to the urge to poke Vadney in an unblinking eye, he showed renewed evidence of sentience: "Neither?"

"What?"

"You said 'neither.'"

"I said 'neither' what?"

Vadney gathered himself up and spoke clearly and cautiously, nearly soberly: "I believe, Camilla, that you said, if I am not mistaken, that, if I heard correctly, that neither 'he,' Nelson, nor 'I,' yourself, one would assume from context, will continue to suffer the something-something of my, that is I, my own, something or other."

He paused. His next words came out on discrete gusts of breath. "You. Will. Be. Leaving?"

"Well, yes, of course I will be leaving. Provided we can save poor Nelson's wracked and tormented soul and deliver him in one functioning, sensate piece to the academy, I will stay near him at Castle Victim, the ancestral seat of Nelson's true father. I could not let him be alone for his years at the school."

Vadney swooned in his chair, the room suddenly spinning around him. His wife continued:

"That is why I have sent your servant to

Boyledin to summon Mistress Blatatat. Despite the low company she keeps and the despicable haunts she is said to frequent, she is known as a seer of great power and an adept guide through the pathways of the spiritual realms. She has quite a reputation. Nelson's soul is at stake. We must have him well enough to travel."

Vadney fell and smacked his drunken head on the marble floor of the hall so forcefully it felt like love.

Cyril puffed on his pipe aggressively, filling the air above him with a soft semaphore of indignation as he listened.

"I don't know what you're so cross

about, Cyril. It makes perfect sense. Besides, I was only following your advice. It's working like a charm, by the way."

"Oh, is it?" Cyril yelped. "I'm so glad! That's really very good news. It's always so nice to feel that you've been able to help a friend — steal food from your own plate!"

"You are being completely melodramatic. You must have known that I'd come to the Jakes sooner or later. It just so happened that it was sooner; and that's in great part due to you, I freely admit that."

"And this is how you show gratitude?"

"Oh, come on, now. Should I have stayed away because you were here? You are always here. When was the last time you didn't perform Amateur Recitation Night? Look, thanks to you in no small part, things are going well for me in Boyledin. I've gotten a reputation. People are talking. But you and I both know how that goes. I've got to make hay while the sun shines."

Cyril stomped the muck in the alley behind the Jakes & Japes. The resultant "squelch" was dissatisfying in the extreme. He turned quickly, intent on kicking something more resounding but lost his boot in the grip of the tenacious filth. The symbolism of being mired in the wet debris behind the tavern in which he'd spent so much of his as-yet inglorious creative life was not lost upon him, meager though his self-awareness might be. He hopped awkwardly on his free foot.

"Is there anything I can do to help?"

"Yes, for pity's sake! Help me get my foot back into my boot! I haven't any other hosiery!"

She assisted him capably, but added, "I meant perhaps something rather more particular to your professional ambitions, Cyril."

Cyril extricated his foot and leapt up to seat himself on a barrel. Seated, he sighed in obvious resignation.

"Look, Cyril. I'll be honest. I've never fully understood what you were on about — I mean when you are onstage. It's energetic and all, but I've never had the faintest sense of what you were talking about or what you were after: shock, applause, thorough confusion? I mean, do you want the audience to like you, to fear you? Remember, these were all questions you told me to answer for myself in that — what was it? — the General . . ."

"The Shakewit General Eminence & Notoriety Index & Usefulness System," Cyril filled in.

"Right. Cyril, it's genius."

"Well, yes, it's called an acronym. When the letters of an abbreviation spell out another recognizable word . . ."

"No, Cyril, you fool. The system itself is genius. It's inspired, filled by the very breath of, well, some muse or another. What I'm saying is that while I've never once understood your act onstage, what you've said about getting to the stage, how to make people want you onstage . . . well, the gods gave you something, Cyril."

"Which, apparently, works best when I give it to you."

"I'm not going to feel bad for you, Cyril. You helped me. Perhaps I can help you. But I'll not wait around, and I'll not be one of those sorry sots stuck at the . . ."

"Stuck belaboring vagrant dreams for the chance of free eel pie and a Daisy drunk every Saturday at the renowned Jakes &

Japes."

"You see things clear enough when you want, Cyril. Perchance you just need to heed a bit of your own counsel: 'No ratty minstrel's cymbals ever crashed so harsh as a well-fed neighbor's lute.'"

"I said that?"

"You did."

"It sounds wise."

"It does."

"Do you know what it means?"

"Not at all."

Cyril gave in. "All right, then. Yes, there is something you can do for me. And, remember, you're the one who said it: You owe me, Tessie."

"It's Ekaterina, now, Cyril. Even for you. Even for you, it's Mistress Ekaterina Blatatat."

The ride from Boyledin was outwardly uneventful: The weather was fair, the carriage in fine repair and the driver of standard skill, which is to say he could be relied upon to hit only those depressions in the road that would cause damage to teeth, bone and nerve and never to horse, freight or flask. For the experienced traveler, certainly, this jaunt out from the capital to the country was no great adventure; but to these passengers it was something exotic and uncertain.

Ratch had made the trip innumerable times. His trips between Boyledin and Isle d'Eaux were in two categories: alone, to deliver a message as to why his master simply could not, honestly, could not possibly, so sorry, best to Nelson, make it back from wherever he was just now; and in the company of his lord, returning to wherever she was at her insistence. These two types had been made, historically, in an exact proportionality, and the difference in the emotional tone of the types had long ago ceased to mean anything to Ratch. The intricacies of his lord and lady's hate-hate relationship had ceased to spark interpretation. Barring broken spokes, bolting horses or highwaymen, one trip was much the same as another. Ratch had grown to routinely crave the intrusion of a highwayman. Or an angry mob of revolutionary peasants. A rude farmer. A belligerent child, formidably tall for his age. A startled badger. Anything between town house and estate that might give him an opportunity to branch out from the terribly proscribed skills of a career domestic and to test his wits or to buckle his swash a bit. So, to be in the company of not one but two unsavory characters — hucksters, charlatans, montebanques, as sure as eggs is eggs — was for Ratch a transporting delight.

At close quarters, Mistress Ekaterina was only a fraction more scrutable than usual. The invitation to the castle was an almost incredible accomplishment and validation. She had worked tirelessly, deliberately crafting her credibility, forging a reputation in the shady margins of the Sink, Boyledin's seediest quarters. Among thieves, gossips, blackmailers, actors, whores, fences, panderers, pickpockets, poisoners, card sharps, conjurers. It was in this low warren of the disadvantaged, decadent and deeply depraved that she could best build a budding legend; for, in socially stratified Maybia, the Sink was a promiscuously shared semi-secret.

Everyone, from urchin to Grand Dauphin, from the courtly to the chancred, has their after-hours appetites. The Sink catered to them all. To be known in the Sink was to be known throughout the realm.

    Ekaterina had walked a fine line in consorting among this element. She had adopted an air of distance and mystery, of otherworldliness. This was appropriate not only to a claimant of supernatural communications, of visions and insights beyond and even through appearances but also to one who would someday sit beside kings and courtiers. She strove to be regarded as in but not of the Sink. The summons of Lady Camilla Fitz-Victim Poon-Grebe was proof positive of her success. The lady was known for her stern correctness. No other noblewoman could so immediately confer an aura of seriousness, of gravity, gravity of an almost grinding force. Lady Poon-Grebe was a veritable pestle of propriety.

This was the very fact that now hopped up and down on Ekaterina's lungs. Lady Camilla's opinions and pronouncements carried the force and traveled the breadth of her own reputation. Ekaterina understood that her ladyship's approval and good report could clad her own regard in ermine and mail; but with a dubious word the noblewoman could condemn her to the workhouse, the stocks or worse: to a life spent hustling the Sink.

Cyril ignored both the enigmatic and semi-rapturous Ratch and the tense silence of Tessie — er, Mistress Blatatat — and gazed through the window of the enclosed carriage. The comfort and sumptuousness of its interior contrasted so harshly with the drabness of the streets of the Sink that Cyril felt resentful at his own pleasure at leaving. If Cyril had been pressed to describe the dominant color of the Sink, he would have said, "cough." How had he lived so long there? And this departure, late as it was, he purchased only by attaching himself to "Ekaterina" through the calling in of favors, the swearing of oaths and the swift talking of nonsense. As ever, Cyril felt that he had swindled himself an advantage he had hoped to earn. An artist before the wrong audience can easily feel a con man.

    Cyril had little hope that Lady Poon-Grebe would be able to offer him his longed-for ovation. Still, the velvet cushions of the carriage were comfortable, and Ratch claimed to have an illuminated folio text of Erroll the Irregular's prison routines. Perhaps something would come up. Plus, he imagined nobles unlikely to express any displeasure by means of frozen produce. It's the little things. As the unremitting grey of Boyledin slowly gave way to the leafier outer settlement and then to the wooded highway, Cyril slipped into sleep to the soft rhythmic panic of Mistress Blatatat, under the pleased and watchful eye of Ratch.

Vadney slumped over the library table, moistening the dry pages of a half-dozen open leather-bound volumes with tears of frustration.

The Wretched Ruby Grimoire, Otto Mondo's Otro Mundo Miscellany, Secrets of the B'Zerki Rhomboids, The Sun Porch of the Scrantic Temple, Tarot for the Addle-pated, The Onandonanonicon. Vadney had torn from his shelves every book he had on the esoteric arts, from alchemy to zoomancy. But not one word in the collection seemed the least bit helpful. He'd hoped to find some sort of introductory passage outlining the basics, something to help him assemble a necromancer's (was that the right term? It wasn't a slur, was it? He was fairly sure that "witch" would be impolite) tool kit: "You'll need a pinch of diced wolf's bane, a linden wand and a bucket of virgin's sweat," that kind of thing. He'd hoped to have serviceable sorcery supplies immediately at hand. No need to waste valuable time scouring the countryside for newts, or what have you. But these infernal infernal books. They all read like the minutes of a county council comprised of hatters and moon children. It was the most formal bit of lunacy Vadney had ever encountered:

"Render unto the thrice-annointed ur-

Underlord (Emeritus) the spoils of Throth, the mons gratuitous of cold-bearing heat damp; yea, too, render unto the Third-Degree Hierolyte, the scimitar, the fennel seed and the egg whisk — not withstanding the presence of the Second-Degree, save he should be possessed of the Goblet of Merkin or clad in the Merkin of Maul, in which case leave out the fennel seed. Thus shall Zigath the Cyclopean Hermaphrodite repose gently till Swiven's Tide, lest the shade of Minette grow bilious."

Vadney felt desperate. He was, he thought, so close to deliverance. Both Camilla and Nelson ensconced tidily away, distantly away, *away* away, at Castle Victim! He could not bear to leave the whole thing up to the suspect skills of a barroom conjurer summoned on some wild whim of his credulous wife.

Personally, Vadney lacked settled notions as to the boundaries of this world and the next, or the natural and the super- . His literary arcana had been selected as much for atmosphere as for actual interest. The afterlife, he thought, was quite purposely named. He had neither fear nor hurry in that regard. But he knew well enough that few residents of the Sink were exactly whom they purported. If this Mistress Blatatat were a fraud . . . It was too terrible to fathom. Vadney would dangle from that bridge when he crossed it. In the meantime, if there were any chance that this woman might help cure Vadney of his own ills by curing Nelson of his, well, he wanted dearly to facilitate such an outcome. Or the sufficient appearance of such. But how?

Did she work with entrails, dice or effigies? Numbers, cauldrons or tea leaves?

Crystal balls or pyromancy? Incantations? Constellations? Bat droppings?

Vadney had worried himself up a great thirst and was reaching to ring for Ratch when he recalled that it was own manservant whom his wife had dispatched to summon this Sink sorceress. That calmed him, though he resented his wife's presumption. He truly hated being without Ratch's comforting capability; but, surely, Ratch would have ample opportunity on the ride back from Boyledin to gather some intelligence, would be able to shed some light on this dark art. Perhaps even enough to give them some slight edge over Camilla, who was relying on the witchy (oops, pardon!) woman's renown, the spooky gossip passed on by the busybody wife of some syphilitic hog of an earl, or another. Maybe Tipsy, Earl of Wangshire, Vadney mused. His wife is a terrible blabbermouth. Oh, no, wait. That was his first wife. She's dead. So, who was he thinking of? Camilla's old friend and recent guest, the former Lady Marionette, had brought that ridiculous continental husband of hers, Lord Sauvignon, the Vicomte de Louche, to court recently and he was a certain habitué of the Sink. Lady Sauvignon was social but subtle, no reckless chatterer; but then again, she was said to have conducted seances at her parties in Puis and she was known to frequent the theater.

Oh, dash it! Vadney slapped shut the open books on the long table. This is getting me nowhere. All I can do is hope that Ratch has gotten the feel of this Blatatat and her methods. I will make available all implements, accoutrements, items, icons and idols she could possibly need. Be it Brusland finery or B'zerki fetish. Whatever. What*ever*, it takes to ensure our endeavor reaches its fruitful conclusion. With his mind settled, his resolve shored, Vadney headed to his wine cellars, quietly, via the back stairs, dying for a more immediate fruitful conclusion.

Castle Grundel loomed. It sprawled. It ranged and bristled and muscled its way around the landscape. Its spires fingered the soft grey clouds, the thick blunt stones of its cellars prodded the earth uncomfortably. Sensitive souls could be moved to sympathetic tears by the castle's rude handling of the verdant environs; the coarse to comments that Mother Nature clearly was asking for it — look how she was arrayed! Isle d'Eaux was lush, ripe, green, soft and accommodating; the Castle

Grundel, severe, brutal, monochromatic and repellent. It was an architecture of perversion and scorn. It projected an air of monumentality and cunning. It seemed somehow both inevitable and sneaky, a devious and politic geology. It was a profoundly unsettling place.

As the carriage left the public road and made its way onto the long and intentionally aggravating causeway that linked Isle d'Eaux to the mainland, Ekaterina opened a hinged glass panel of the near window to gaze forward at their destination. Her expression betrayed her and Ratch spoke for the first time in many minutes, catching her by surprise.

"It does take some getting used to."

"What?" Ekaterina said, more out of surprise than incomprehension.

"This. The castle. The approach. Many,

most, find it unpleasant initially, or longer. It was designed that way, for better or worse."

"This is on purpose?"

"The first Marquis d'Isle d'Eaux was an ingenious man."

"Lord Leslie designed this, himself?"

Ratch raised an eyebrow appreciatively. "You know some history, then."

"Well, yes." Ekaterina was careful to maintain what of her placid demeanor remained, but she bristled inwardly at the hint that Ratch might think her ignorant. "Little scholarship enough is needed to know the family Poon-Grebe."

"Hmmm," the servant murmured noncommittally. "And, yet, one can always be surprised to discern what others know that they have little reason to know, or those things of which they are ignorant despite title, claim or reputation."

Ekaterina kept Ratch's gaze: "Indeed. One might resolve never to underestimate one's acquaintances or overestimate one's self, mightn't one?"

"One might," Ratch's smile was large and perplexingly genuine seeming. Yet, it hit Ekaterina in her already-fluttering gut like a sulfurous sack lunch of aged eggs. "The way straightens in a moment. To allow the archers a clear line of fire."

And so it did, allowing Ekaterina the merciful equilibrium to sit silently with Ratch, allowing the color to return to her face. In the last yards, as the carriage approached the gatehouse, neither spoke. As they clattered to a stop and waited for the massive portcullis to be raised from within, Ratch exhaled wistfully.

"There are, of course, no archers now. They're hardly necessary in this day and age. And, frankly, even the inhospitable approach is probably superfluous."

"How does one keep out the undesirable, then" Ekaterina asked archly.

Ratch's laugh was sudden, full and guileless.

"Oh, by keeping them in!"

His lingering chuckles were lost in the grating rasp as the barred barrier was winched away. The screeching roused Cyril, who had slept heavily and not spoken nor stirred from the moment the carriage cleared the city's limits. He yawned loudly and stretched, craning his neck to peer around through the windows.

"A little heavy on the foreboding for my taste, but I guess home is where you hang your heraldry, huh?" He turned to face Ekaterina, who was gazing at the enormous soot-colored stones of the castle's formidable walls and snaggled battlements. She thought suddenly, anxiously, irrationally, "What if this noble brat really is possessed?"

"Are you well, Mistress Blatatat?" Cyril asked ingratiatingly. "You look like you've seen a ghost."

Ekaterina turned an implacable gaze upon him.

"Well, have you?" he wheedled, sweetly.

She held his gaze without comment or flinch. Her face was expressionless. He began forming another ironic nicety, discarded it as too mild and busied with another. Preoccupied as he was with this self-satisfied mental fumbling, he was taken quite by surprise when Ekaterina's eyes rolled back into her head and her body tremored so that it shook the carriage on its creaking axles.

"St. Jasper's rash!" he swore.

Ekaterina's left arm rose toward the men as if on a pulley. Her index finger trembled up and outward. She seemed to be indicating a spot between them, spasming first toward Ratch then toward Cyril. Her jaw dropped and with only the slightest movement of her lips she croaked:

The swine, well-bred and well-fed
is ousted from his pen.
The orangutan, raised on piggy's back
to ride away on him.
Perigee and apogee,
apex, then the zenith.
Who can tell just which is which
Or the nitwit from the genius?

She collapsed backward against the lush upholstery of the seat, a light glaze of sweat shining on her forehead and upper lip.

Ratch and Cyril stared at her, then one another. Chivalry resurfaced as shock subsided and they leaned forward to steady the rousing Mistress Blatatat. Holding her at the elbows, they assisted her into the open air of the courtyard where they were met by valets who scuttled about, retrieving luggage, and a footman who nodded to Ratch then led the way into the castle. As Ekaterina crunched after the guide, Ratch and Cyril followed.

"It's really quite an act, you've got to admit," Ratch said.

"Oh, shut up," said Cyril.

They approached the pair of mammoth oak doors opened wide in a block archway. Ekaterina paused only briefly, then stepped confidently into Castle Grundel, Cyril and Ratch close behind. They passed through the intimidating maw of the doorway into an even more overwhelming anteroom. "More like 'gigante-room,' right?" Cyril said seemingly to no one. The walls were soaring dark walnut and joined the distant ceiling at moldings of timbers both heavy and intricately carved. The floors were of exotic ebony wood burnished to such a high shine they reflected back to him every mismatched and colorful patch of his oft-mended garments. It was a vast and frighteningly beautiful space that gave Cyril the impression of plummeting from the lofty decks of a Viperian war ship to the nighttime depths of the Gaspian Sea.

"It's no wonder the nobility are so often found taking their entertainment at the Jakes," Cyril said. "I'd not be eager to come home either, if this were my welcoming entrance."

"Nobility do not enter here, I assure

you," said Ratch. "This is the servant's entrance. The others make a bolder impression."

"What, like a bear pit?"

Ratch did not respond, conferring as he was with another member of the Poon-Grebe house staff. So, Cyril turned his attention to Mistress Blatatat.

"Your routine should go over well, here," he said quietly. "Loads of atmosphere, and all. Look, I'll admit to being a little put out by your win at the Jakes. No hard feelings, but I was in a competitive frame of mind. I think I couldn't really see then that you've worked up something special. And in this setting? Your bit in the carriage had me going, I'll not lie."

"My bit in the carriage?"

"Yeah, the spooky stuff."

"I got a little light-headed, was all. I

appreciate your great gallantry helping me down a single carriage step but if that's your idea of 'spooky' . . ."

"No, not that! The poem! The eyeballs! The finger!"

Ekaterina regarded him quizzically. "You don't travel well, do you?"

Cyril sputtered. "I? Wait! No." He fluttered his hands around like startled birds, casting glances back through the doorway toward the courtyard, toward the carriage, in part for dramatic emphasis and in part to retrace his own steps, to verify his experience. Throughout, Ekaterina watched him with a curious expression. Was she genuinely puzzled or secretly amused?

"Ah, ok, " Cyril said, letting his hands and his head drop in an attitude of submission. "Fine. Very good. Nicely done. Excellently, in fact. No denying it. You've got a knack for this. I'm not too proud to admit that I'm impressed. I mean, this ain't my first time at the tournament, you know? But, still. Very sweetly done. But in the end, as they say, 'there's no jestin' the jester.' "

"Fool."

"Oh, is it? Ok. 'There's no foolin' the fool.' "

Ekaterina turned as she spoke. "You had the expression right the first time."

Ahead by several steps, Ratch beckoned them forward through a succession of functional rooms: kitchens and storerooms, larders and pantries, all stocked to bursting: casks, vats, hogsheads, barrels, bags and baskets; shelves and ceilings woven with nets of cured meats and cheeses. It was like a merchant caravan, carrying an order of absolutely everything. The surplus made Cyril's head spin. There were at this moment, in this castle, more provisions than had passed over his own family's tables in the previous three generations (this was a bit of license on Cyril's part, as he could only reliably trace back his ancestry one generation). There were spoons in Castle Grundel, he speculated, with more august histories than he had himself.

"Spoons," he spat.

"Pardon?" Ratch asked, turning his head without stopping. Clearly, in a hallway of such length it was important to maintain forward progress. Who knew what might roam these halls by night. Wouldn't do to get lost.

"Bread crumbs," Cyril barked.

"Ah, yes," said Ratch, affirmatively.

The servants who had met them and accompanied them along their circuitous route through the work areas (Lord Leslie had hoped to frustrate any easy escape with his snacks, as well, it appeared) dropped away from their party en route. After this thoroughly discombobulating and appetite-stimulating march, they were just three at the bottom of a stone stairwell curved along the rough, bulky inner wall of an enormous turret. After the sensuous tour through the castle's stores, this was a reminder of its fundamental ugliness and of the inhabiting family's somewhat bi-polar legend of historic accomplishment and offense, of both nation building and alarming nuttiness, of moment and "hey, now, wait a moment!"

But then all great men are a bit bats, Cyril thought, not entirely without admiration. Still though, unpredictable men of significant mood swings were often noted as "great" by those with the softened perspective of having not been murdered by them.

"Hey, Ratch. This is some tower. You're not leading us to the dungeon, are you?"

"Of course not," came the calm response. "No one with any sense puts a dungeon in a tower. It's too easy for guests to leap to their deaths. Ours is in the basement."

Cyril's pace slowed and he briefly lost sight of his companions as they rounded an upper curve. But Ratch's voice reached him, lilting, chill and echoey:

"No one likes a spoil sport."

"When did everyone get so annoyingly funny?" Cyril wondered, and heavily trudged up the tower stairs.

The mere existence of a "dining room" in a private residence in Maybia indicated an unusual affluence and architectural abundance. In Boyledin, the teeming and closely packed capital, the greater portion dined in taverns and eating establishments of greatly variable quality and ambience: the comfortable (the comfort of inherited position or predatory wiles) in private clubs of exacting elegance; the masses in homelier accommodations, from humble to horrifying. In the countryside, whole families supped in the very same room in which they mended their rugs and beat their children, or vice versa.

The dedicated dining area in either town or country was statistically rare and conceptually challenging: an entire chamber excepted from the normal function of the home save this one specific, simple task —

chewing. Imagine!

It may go without saying, then, that neither Cyril nor Ekaterina were familiar with even the luxury of a entry-level residential dining room, that of a successful dye merchant or a retired buccaneer with a house-proud, foreign-born wife, for example. Had they been, they would still have been prodigiously unready for the dining hall at Castle Grundel.

In fairness to these overwhelmed guests, "hall" is hardly apt. It's just a categorical commonplace. "Amphitheater," even "arena" might be closer to usefully descriptive. Those words better approach the scale of the room, as well as hint at the sense growing within Cyril and Ekaterina that the opportunities and risks, both, were unlike any they had been presented before. Had it been announced that tonight's menu and guest list were one and the same, had Ratch opened the dining-room doors like the side of an ark to admit live and famished beasts of prey, wished them all "good luck" and "good eating" without any indication at all as to which species he spoke, well, Cyril and Ekaterina might have been stricken but not, precisely speaking, surprised. But for the moment, they stood uncertainly in the hall, alone.

"Do you think that's a chandelier up there? Or is it — what's the constellation? — the Girdle of Phillipa? I can't quite tell if there's ceiling," Cyril said, craning his neck.

Ekaterina neither responded nor looked up. She was, in fact, strangely immobile. She was dressed simply but elegantly, Cyril noticed. He assumed that her garments had been provided, as had his own new and rather flashier outfit, by their as-yet unmet hosts. It struck him that he had nearly forgotten how pretty she was. He was surprised to realize how he had, despite himself, begun to accept the transformation of Tessie Trewes into the enigmatic Ekaterina Blatatat. But here, in this cavernous castle hall, shorn, as it were, of her accoutrements and mystery she looked again the Boyledin urchin, however pretty.

"Ekaterina. Ekaterina. Tessie!" Cyril hissed.

She started. She turned toward him as if only just now noticing that she'd been accompanied into the room.

"Cyril . . ." she left off.

"You look terrified. You've got to pull it together."

"What . . . ?" Ekaterina was barely present.

"Now!" Cyril half ran, half crept to the

doors, listening. "They could be here at any moment!"

"You were brought here at the specific request — the request, not the command — of Lady Camilla Fitz-Victim Poon-Grebe. You are Mistress Ekaterina Blatatat, most powerful seer in Boyledin, in all of Maybia! And winner of the Amateur Recitation Night of the most venerable Jakes & Japes! Don't forget. You are Mistress Ekaterina Blatatat. Be Mistress Ekaterina Blatatat."

Ekaterina straightened, and patted her hair. Cyril thought that she paused slightly and smiled at him with warmth, but it was so fleeting he began to distrust that thought: Mistress Blatatat exuded no perceptible warmth. "St. Garrick's gout, it's a convincing routine." Cyril suddenly felt as distant from her as he did from the chandelier, or whatever it was hanging over them.

"The Lady Camilla Fitz-Victim Poon-Grebe," announced Ratch as he opened the doors inward. He executed a deft pirouette, somehow securing both heavy paneled doors gracefully while assuming a position against the inner wall, clearing the way for the Marchioness d'Isle d'Eaux.

It could not be said (well, it could not be said sincerely) of Lady Poon-Grebe that she was graceful. But neither was she clumsy, which implies distraction and accident. Lady Poon-Grebe instead moved as if unruly chance had been duly chastised and sent to its room. The scientists and philosophers of Maybia's prestigious Society for Meta-Illumnative Research and Knowledge had fortunately never been faced with the sight of the lady navigating her way from point A to point B. Had they, the blow to inquiry would have been tremendous: They would surely have abandoned not only their favorite theory of the moment, the Pluralistic Presents Model of Every- and Otherthingness, but also a basic belief in any points other than A and B. Lady Camilla walked and possibility collapsed in her wake.

The universe, however (or *this* universe, if you happen to be a S.M.I.R.K. researcher, yourself) conspires toward chaos.

"Lord Vadney Poon-Grebe," called Ratch, and in careened the 13th marquis in full regalia, to stand beside his wife. Looking at them, Ekaterina thought she sensed some specific incarnation of the fundamental dichotomies of existence, of dark and light, good and evil, of appetite and idealism, but she could not say which represented which, or what animated whom. Cyril, looking at them, thought of a vulgar rhyme:

Glutton ate his button because he had no meat
   and then his pants fell down a-rising from his seat.
   Milady refused gravy in a fit of pique,
   then complained of dryness with Glutton's arse caught in her beak.

He stifled a laugh. He'd never really had any idea what the chant — popular with the dirty children of the Sink — was supposed to mean. He'd have a hard time articulating it now, frankly. But somehow it seemed slightly less nonesensical.

Lady Poon-Grebe made her way (or rather the way wisely opened before Lady Poon-Grebe) and she closed the distance between herself and Ekaterina. The women faced each other with no greeting for moments, as Cyril looked on nervously. Should she take the marchioness's hand, he fretted. In his upset, he himself curtsied. But no one seemed to notice. After what to him seemed an epoch, the women nodded to each other.

"Welcome, Mistress Blatatat. We are honored and much relieved to receive you here at Castle Grundel."

"You are most gracious, my lady. I only hope that my abilities may benefit and comfort you and your family."

"That is kind of you, Mistress. But you must be ravenous. Please, let us be seated."

Servants streamed silently and fluidly into and through the room, like a school of formal fish. They were behind each chair before the intended occupant arrived.

Throughout the sumptuous meal, platters appeared and were spirited away, drinks were refilled and exchanged wholly with each course as if the very furniture and flatware were sentient. "No wonder so many noblemen seemed total feather heads," thought Cyril. "There's no need for them to think, at all!"

Engaged in conversation with the lady of the castle, Ekaterina was having a different experience of Maybian aristocracy. Whatever else she might be — credulous, gullible, superstitious, Ekaterina was hopeful for some advantage — Lady Poon-Grebe was not dimwitted. Ekaterina wondered uncomfortably if she had, if she would need, allies. She glanced toward the men at the table: Cyril across from her, Lord Vadney to her right. Though she knew Cyril to be possessed of an erratic kind of quasi-genius and she knew the marquis to be a direct descendent of a long line of heroes, at this moment she saw only a sliver of such resources. Cyril was speaking around a mouthful of painstakingly prepared, delicately flavored food, the complex nuances of which he obliterated entirely by the haste and capacity of his spoonwork. Lord Vadney was staring in a wholly not-aristocratic fashion, Ekaterina thought, straight back at her. She despaired.

"Excellent fare, your lordship," Cyril smacked. "The hospitality of Castle Grundel is insufficiently celebrated. It's as fine as the castle itself is ferocious. Really marvelous. Her ladyship runs, as they say, 'a tidy frigate.'"

Lord Poon-Grebe had a slowly settling realization that he was being spoken to and turned with evident reluctance toward the moist noise.

"Sorry. What?"

Pitching his voice to carry more successfully the length of the table, Cyril restated, "The welcome you have extended us is exquisite, as is your residence. Our appreciation and compliments are yours."

It was Lady Poon-Grebe who responded. "I abhor this indulgent luxury and find this monstrous edifice repugnantly vainglorious. It is my husband's family seat and the residence of myself and my dear afflicted son only in painful fact, not fittingness. That is the reason, the urgent cause, for which I sought you, Mistress Blatatat."

Quietly, Lord Poon-Grebe added, "It's nice of you to say, though."

Lady Camilla continued, speaking directly and for all appearances exclusively to Ekaterina: "Mistress Blatatat, word has reached me by way of a most reliable friend, a dear friend of great spiritual sensitivity..."

"I knew it!" thought Vadney. "That weirdo, Lady Sauvignon!"

"... who advises me that you have the gift to light the dark recesses of the soul, to peer into the mazy depths and discern both hazard and true path toward the light of right and higher being, to guide those who have been waylaid through weakness..."

Vadney shifted uncomfortably under his wife's sudden regard.

"... or set upon by the ever-watchful and opportunistic legions of both corporeal and spectral vice and villainy, by action or by influence."

Mistress Blatatat (for surely it was she, the famed spiritualist, who now spoke) answered in a clear and steady voice that, though unstrained, resounded.

"I have, my lady, essayed practices long abandoned by most. I have studied arts arcane, incomprehensible and unknown to even the most celebrated of our scientists, scholars and surgeons. I have sacrificed and suffered to align my apprehension away from the common course and, thus, I see and may sometimes describe the uncommon and the rarely seen but ever-present. If I may be of help to you in this way, I place myself in your service."

Lady Poon-Grebe's face assumed a position that Vadney knew to be a smile, though few others would have labeled it as such.

"You cannot know the comfort and hope you have offered me, Mistress Blatatat, for you see, my boy . . ."

"Forgive me, your ladyship," Ekaterina

interrupted. "While I must hear aspects of your experience, I can see that this pains you to recount, and I would spare you the discomfort of expounding upon that which I may readily behold."

Mistress Blatatat rose from her chair, breathing in deeply and extending her arms slightly from her sides as she did. The effect was much as if she had levitated, and Cyril dropped his hand before finishing a full gesture and was left with a spoon protruding from his mouth beneath wide eyes.

"I cannot believe how good she has gotten at this," he marveled to himself.

Vadney, too, was wide-eyed and caught up in private admiration, but let's just leave it at that.

Ekaterina left her place at the table and softly prowled the room's extensive perimeter, trailing her hand along its dark wood-paneled wall. The seated trio scooted their chairs counterclockwise to watch her as she circled behind them.

"This is an ancient place," Ekaterina said. "More ancient than Maybia, itself, we know. History dwells here. Not as a pin in a map, but as an active if unseen occupant. All that has been here, is here still, ever asserting, ever contending, ever exerting, ever demanding."

Vadney thought of the gallery leading to his library and swallowed a goblet of wine.

"Many places are so occupied, but few so forcefully. Castle Grundel is, your lord- and ladyship, a full and raging cataract in the current of time. Nelson is currently but a frail vessel on this riotous confluence."

"Oh, but can he be saved?" Lady Poon-Grebe moaned.

Mistress Blatatat did not address the question immediately but walked several steps more to stop directly behind Lord Poon-Grebe's high-backed chair at the head of the table. She placed her hands on either side of the chair, bracketing Vadney, who froze entirely.

"No. No one can be saved, my lady. But we may, may, correct his course. And, as we all are borne on this current, by righting Nelson's path we may, too, clear the progress of others or ourselves."

Cyril clapped twice before catching himself and pushing his hands under the table like a man resetting a Jack-in-the-Box.

Lord Poon-Grebe stirred as Ekaterina returned to her own chair, and took a long shuddering draft from his refilled wine glass, like a man recently pulled from a chilly, falls-bound river.

"Mistress Blatatat, please be assured that anything you need, anything at all, will be provided without question or delay and that if you can restore my dear boy to himself, to me, there is no end to the gratitude I would be too glad to show you. We will let you rest and gather strength from your journey to us, and hope that you will begin this mission of mercy and righteousness at your earliest preference tomorrow."

"I'm a bit of a late riser . . ."

"I would be pleased to wake you, myself, Mistress . . ."

Cyril and Vadney spoke over one another, thereby garbling the intent of each, which, judging from the looks of the silent women, may have been the earliest act of mercy performed during this intervention.

Cyril stood before the long looking-glass, long looking at himself. Such ogling he lavished on his reflection as would spur the suspicion of constables and the ire of husbands throughout Maybia were it employed in public.

"And this is how they dress indoors. For bed," he muttered, turning to admire himself from a slightly different angle. Ratch had left the rose-petal-pink silk pajama suit, the crimson brocade-and-velvet dressing gown and the soft slippers (with elaborate heraldic embellishments) for him, with his lordship's compliments. Cyril allowed himself the thought that he was merely playing along, inhabiting a role in this as-yet undefined project of opportunism; he scoffed mildly as he slid (yes, slid) into the exotic, almost lurid, fabric: "Preposterous," he huffed.

But that disdain detached itself completely by the time he knotted the golden rope-like sash around his waist, noticing how its color corresponded to the emblems on his toes. The class critique, now loose and free of its object, hovered briefly in a confused flutter, then attached itself to every homely and more-familiar garment Cyril had ever worn before today. What had seemed garish and impractical and even obscenely ornamental struck him now as fine and specific and appropriate. "Context," he announced to himself, looking around the grand bed chamber.

He recalled the chastisement (for it was, he realized now, a chastisement) that Ekaterina offered him: His narrow view of the world had led him to obsess about the Jakes & Japes Amateur Recitation Night as the one route out of the Sink. Yet it had also simultaneously prevented the attainment of the goal. He hadn't been able to see beyond that step. Whereas, Ekaterina, fortunately for him, had. Cyril wondered what she saw next. He, himself, could not envision clearly a discrete, concrete goal. But he resolved there and then to never again deny the possibility of grander things momentarily beyond his imagination. He would, he promised, live up to these glorious pajamas.

And what would the habitual wearer of such night dress do after dinner, belly full and contemplative? A smoke and a stroll. Cyril rooted through his original, and now faintly contemptible, rags, and found his pipe and his pouch. He packed his familiar blend and lit it from the fireplace with a straw plucked from the hearthside whisk. He watched the smoke blossom into the room, feeling as he did that he, too, expanded into the space, occupied it more fully. He was eager to stake his spurious smoky claim elsewhere. He left the chamber and struck out down the hall, scent marking his way through the ancient, famous castle with thick puffs of Ginger Orphan, the cheapest, harshest tobacco known in the Sink.

He set out uncertainly. The castle's layout remained completely opaque and illogical to him. More evidence of Lord Leslie's antagonistic instincts, Cyril assumed. But clad in his nighttime finery, Cyril felt softly armored, comfortably shuffling (slippers were an unfamiliar skill) through the chilly vaults and passages as if a long-time resident content of any destination within.

After many ascents and descents on staircases of marble, staircases of granite, staircases of lushly carpeted wood, after terraces, balconies and turrets, after one smoking chamber with billiard table, two empty ballrooms and a curiously located cast-iron roll-top bath tub, Cyril found himself in a long gallery with regularly spaced niches in which hung portraits of the most off-putting aspects.

"Yeesh," Cyril thought, and as he walked the row of terrible paintings he found they got no yeeshier in the slightest. In fact, it was just that, the consistency, the uninterrupted flow of startling yeeshiness that was most striking about this procession of figures, positioned opposite east-facing windows as if to scare all the art in all the museums across the Poon into polite submission behind velvet ropes. Though details of costume and context varied, indicating the passage of the generations, the family line was easily followed: The faces were severe and merciless. The early bearded titans were no less foxlike in their look of cunning, the later clean-shaven no less virile in their will. They were epochal characters, forces of, rather than figures from, history.

The "yeesh" was threatening to turn to "yuck," and unsettle Cyril's bedclothes-induced sense of lordly leisure when his eyes grasped relief. Here was a face of less nerve-twinging quality: similarly vulpine as those before but more skittish than sly; and if there were anything of the barbarian in this one it was vestigial. It was a clever and comforting caricature of the previous twelve, and relieved Cyril of this mounting upset. Until it spoke.

Given the nearly frictionless quality of the pajamas, it was perhaps only the secure knot in the sash that kept him from shooting upward through the sleeping suit, beyond the robe's shawl collar and into scandal and shame. He started so violently that, in turn, the speaker yelled, leapt backward and disappeared suddenly. As Cyril's heart slowed to a mere rapid tattoo, he gazed into the niche he had assumed contained an 13th family portrait and saw the heavy blank face of a stately door in its jamb.

When he felt sufficiently composed to deliver a controlled knock he rapped twice. After a pause and a high squeak and a noise like a small dog barking and a throat-clearing whine, a voice thinly called, "Yes?"

"Lord Poon-Grebe?"

"Yes. It is I."

"My lord, it's Cyril. Cyril Shakewit. With Ek . . . With Mistress Blatatat? From dinner?"

"Ah, yes. Of course. Dinner. Very good. Yes."

Cyril was not at all sure of how to proceed. The basic fact of being in the castle of a marquis was mind-bogglingly unprecedented for him; to have cornered said marquis in an obscure chamber of his own aforementioned castle while clad in the man's spare pajamas after mistaking him for a droll cartoon of his horrific ancestors . . . Well, that was rather beyond beyond.

"Uh . . . Did I startle you, my lord?"

"What? Oh, no. No. Not at all. I just forgot something. Just forgot something in here. Oh, and, yes, here it is, right here. Silly thing. How amusing. Yes."

"I'm quite sorry. I was just fitful after dinner and thought to admire your home, which is so striking. We saw rather little of it when we arrived. The kitchens and the turret stairway . . . I joked with Ratch about a dungeon and he had a bit of fun with me . . ."

The door swung open and once again Cyril was face to face with the current Maquis d'Isle d'Eaux.

"Do you have an interest in dungeons?"

Ekaterina held herself inches above the thick rugs of the bed chamber with only her palms, legs crossed in front of her. She had not blinked in three minutes and seventeen seconds. She also had not drawn a breath in that time, and her heart rate had slowed to a point as to be, if not entirely undetectable, sluggish enough to test the patience of anyone waiting. People more evidently vital in that regard had gone under the morticians brush and the sod of city cemeteries — if rumors are to be believed.

But Ekaterina was not ailing. The exertions of bodily control were part of a practice, elements of a deliberate routine. In these and other ways she had trained herself to be uncommon. Her body did not seem to make the same demands upon her as most do upon their respective residents; rather her's seemed singularly responsive to her demands upon it.

Such oddity in the name of vision was not utterly unknown in the land. Word of esoteric orders and cults and covens delighted the curious and the condescending: the Eel Priests of Dampnia, the city of canals; the Malfromagians of St. Gruyere Abbey outside Puis, whose ecstatic visions were possible only due to an exclusive diet of powerful beer and spoiled cheese; the Twirling Hurlers of B'zerk, who spin for hours, or days, to produce prophetic projectile vomit the patterns of which they read with eerie accuracy. And within the borders of Maybia, itself, there were communities of mystic discipline: the contortionist Knot Witches of the Warren of Horn; the zealots known as the Cubists, who built themselves into tiny boxes of beautiful design and flawless craftsmanship; the followers of the High Priestess Aerobia, who performed elaborate ritualized and coordinated movements in private rooms till they collapsed of dehydration, all in time with small bands of musicians playing popular drinking songs of the day.

  Ekaterina's practice had been spawned by practicality not doctrine, though. She had neither an inherited nor a personal theology. What philosophy she might be pressed to articulate was less eschatological than economic. She believed most fiercely in the importance of not starving and of becoming increasingly less filthy. It was clear to her from a young age, observant as she was, that this likely meant getting out of the perpetually belly-rumbling, soot-and-shit-smearing Sink.

In cultivating her reputation, much at Cyril's prodding, she had seized upon the need to present some apprehensible marker of difference. The credible seers of Maybia all were in some way distinguished as "other." A common way was to be notably learned and read in the esoteric literature, the eldritch canon. But that was a costly route best available to the frail progeny of nobility. Another was to be raving mad, but even as Tessie Trewes, she had possessed a certain gravitas that hampered such antics. Ekaterina knew intuitively that her opportunity lay in sternness, in mettle. She set out to master herself and to use that self-possession as a tool for other types of possession. Driven, she worked toward control over the tools most readily available, her body and will. Though not advertised as such, for obvious reasons, Ekaterina was Maybia's one and only agnostic mystic, a self-made faker fakir.

This was not the handicap one might presume. Doubt-ridden clergy, now, there's a crisis in the making: Administrative efficiency suffers from open-minded ecclesiastics. A respectable crusade, for example, does not admit an "on the other hand," unless the other is, too, wielding a slicing, bludgeoning or, at least, moderately scourging weapon. But as a freelance, so to speak, Ekaterina could be more receptive and less judgmental of the welter of jury-rigged faiths, the frothy folklore, the panic-edged superstitions and the mercurial existential insights of Maybia's credulous. It broadened her client base, generously.

She had developed an instinctual, body-based type of rigorous unbelief, free from existing dogma. Her audiences brought to her their prejudices, their precepts, their presuppositions and she took them all, spun them on their axes and gave them back, largely unchanged, save the significant surcharge. Though she bristled at the term, downplaying as it did the effort and application required, she privately agreed with Cyril that it has become a "heckuva racket." But recently things had gotten complicated.

Ekaterina blinked slowly, soothing her smarting eyes. She lowered herself to the floor, breathing deeply, then stood. She glanced at herself only briefly in her dressing mirror. She had long ago lost fascination with the athletic boyishness her discipline had given her body (another distinction of hers among the plump and fleshy ideal of Maybian femininity). She pulled on the simple sleeping dress left for her by one of Lady Poon-Grebe's unspeaking maids. She knew it would be best to sleep. But her mind was, unusually, a hive of frantic thought.

The Poon-Grebes' need was an incredible opportunity for Ekaterina. But Nelson's affliction troubled her. Why? The castle was unsettling; the history and prominence of its residents almost more so. But there was, Ekaterina knew, something other making her obedient heart unruly. Ekaterina was nervous.

In recent performances, she had felt herself drifting. Not through boredom or inattention. She was too professional and too well-trained for that to be the case. But as if pulled on an external current, transported. She'd had . . . visions. At sessions' ends she had been surprised to hear clients repeat back to her pronouncements she could not quite remember making. Ekaterina's trancelike states had become actual trances. It was not so much that Ekaterina worried that her clients would stop believing in her oracular utterances as she was terrified that she would start. The loss of control was extremely worrisome.

 She knew she needed sleep, and she knew it would not come. She also knew that her one resource was, as had so mysteriously been the case before (she shook her head), Cyril.

 Ekaterina pulled on the hefty,

undecorated robe left for her and headed into the hallway, hopeful to find Cyril's chamber in this grim maze before dawn.

"This is horrifying!"

Lord Poon-Grebe's face flushed.

"It's terrible!"

He took a deep breath and closed his eyes, rapturously.

"It's . . . It's depraved!"

Vadney spoke with barely suppressed emotion, "You're not just saying that to be polite?"

Cyril swept open his arms to indicate the entirety of Vadney's well-stocked dungeon. "Absolutely not! This is the finest, most impressive dungeon I've ever beheld! I'd say this is convincing testimony to an inspired and dangerous imagination!"

"Have you seen many dungeons?"

"Well, not as such, no. But then you needn't sample all the fare to know a feast when you see one, wouldn't you agree? This dungeon, my lord, is a nightmare."

As Cyril spoke, Lord Poon-Grebe seem to increase in height, an elevation only checked when Cyril enquired, "So, was this the work of Lord Leslie Poon-Grebe, too?"

"What?" Vadney cried out. "No! It is my own!"

"You, my lord? All this? Everything?"

"Well, yes. Leslie's energies tended to the more public displays. Battlefields, and whatnot. So, this is my handicraft."

"Even the tapestries?"

"Do you find them un-dungeonlike?"

"No, no. I like them. They cut the chill. A fellow could catch his death down here."

Cyril ambled about the room, investigating the various implements and engines, tugging at straps with hefty buckles in apparent admiration, rapping an ominous hollow boom on the side of a large brass vat in the shape of cattle, admiring a leather-clad hinged case of myriad whips and flails. Vadney beamed throughout.

"If it's not impertinent to note, my lord . . ." Cyril began.

"Yes?"

"Well, these devices — all of great knee-quaking impression — are in quite remarkably pristine condition."

"Yes. Ratch was instructed to be exacting and scrupulous in acquisition. He's really very competent, you know."

"Indubitably, my lord. One senses it immediately upon meeting him. But what I was getting at, is that the dungeon seems, pardon my likely ignorance of dungeon care and maintenance, rather more artfully arranged than actively engaged, as it were."

"I'm not sure I follow you, Mr. Shakewit."

(To be called "Mister" by a lord! But he pressed on.)

"I am sure that it is none of my concern and it is only my delight and admiration at such skill in the creation of this tableau of terror that pushes me to question, my lord. But these nefarious properties seem . . . unused."

"Ahh, yes." Vadney shifted uncomfortably on his feet. "Well, I've only just put the finishing touches on the place, you see? And what with the Nelson situation, there's been such distraction. And, honestly, it wouldn't do to introduce just any blockhead into this — one who wouldn't know a Brazen Bull from a butter churn. It's so hard to find appreciative company."

"Of course, my lord. I understand completely."

"You do?"

"I believe I do. I mean no presumption, but if I may hazard a theory?"

"By all means, sir. Please do!"

("Sir"!)

"You are, my lord, a member of what is unquestionably the most prestigious noble family of all Maybia. The exploits, adventures and conquests of your forebears are those of the country, herself. They are, without exaggeration, legendary. But those were different times, my lord. Unsubtle times. Unrefined times, if I may."

"Yes, quite so, quite so," Vadney said warmly.

"The battlefields of today are rather more metaphorical. The great men of our age are more likely to wield pens than pikes, to turn a phrase."

"It's true," Vadney nodded enthusiastically.

"You, Lord Vadney, are a man of great family, a man of great name. But you are also a man of your age. It takes little enough observation to see that you are no barbarian."

"I like to think I have some taste."

"Exquisite taste, my lord. Exquisite! This dungeon is likely the most divinely appointed and arranged in Maybia, in history!"

"Oh, that is kind."

Cyril had ratcheted up his rhetoric to a high pitch, now he quieted.

"The Poon-Grebe family has provided preeminent men in every generation since its founding. There is no reason why that distinguished tradition should cease in this era."

"No?"

"No. What your martial ancestors accomplished in rapacity, you may accomplish, my lord, in reputation, a tool as powerful in our day as the mortar in theirs, as precise and fine in our hands as the rapier in theirs."

"I do like how that sounds, I must say! But how do I do such a thing?"

"If I may be so bold, my lord, I believe I may be your man. I have some G.E.N.I.U.S., you see."

Ekaterina wondered how long it would take were she to reside in such a place for her to acclimate to its spaciousness; or, for that matter, were its residents forced to dwell in the reeky closeness of the Sink, for them to be driven around the bend, around the three following bends and then again around the original out of sheer desperation.

    She was uncertain how long she'd wandered. Time itself seemed elastic and elongated in these unending halls. But the forced directionlessness, rather than frustrating her, had proved a balm to her nerves. She was not native to such grandeur; she was still overwhelmed and disoriented. But Ekaterina's ambition was itself a sprawling and well-fortified thing. The more she traveled the twists of Castle Grundel, the more she occupied it, the more she felt she could, the more she felt she should. The interior space of the ranging structure felt to her like the first inhalation after one of her breathless routines. It came first as a gasp, almost panicked, then as a sustaining elixir brewed by deliberate deprivation. She had held her breath for years in the close quarters of Boyledin's poorest district. She'd resisted an imagination-and-expectation stunting crush. She'd contested the indoctrination of "survive and scrabble" and adopted a countervailing drive toward transformation and triumph.

Little matter that she did not yet know the specifics of her goal any more than she knew the layout of this confounding castle. Her surety, now restored, reordered the space around her, making her its central point. Once again, Ekaterina felt deliberate and purposeful. She was not certain of the purpose but she was certain it was her own.

She was also certain that her earlier instinct to seek out Cyril was still valid — though Cyril himself was a kind of anti-purpose. Ekaterina felt herself sometimes to be motivated as if on rails, rails that converged at a distant vanishing point on the horizon. The ultimate destination was hidden and inevitable. Cyril seemed to travel as if by ricochet. He was inventive, innovative, charismatic in his clumsy fashion, and lacking in discernible direction almost altogether. Cyril's progress, his very thought process, was like a flock of birds suddenly taking flight in a great spiraling cloud of complexity, precision and grace only to land, en masse, exactly, inexplicably, six inches to the left of their original roost. It was beautiful and bizarre.

 Erratic as his imagination was, it brought him places few others could reach. You would, yourself, no doubt, merely step the six inches to the left, like a reasonable and efficient person. Ekaterina knew that she would, as well. But you and she would therefore miss the feel of the winds' currents, the fine spray of moisture in the air, the varying qualities of light at height and the perspective on the side-stepping masses that this elaborate and seemingly unnecessary flight of fancy provided. Cyril was a baffling ally, but valuable.

In her reverie, Ekaterina had roamed a great distance without finding obvious evidence of her fellow guest or her hosts. She was pleased then — after an initial shock — to find Ratch standing in still anticipation in a chamber full of exotic taxidermy animals.

"I apologize for startling you, Mistress. It was my observation that you might be searching for something."

"Quite all right, Ratch. Yes, I was looking for Mr. Shakewit and I suppose I got a bit lost in thought — and in fact."

"Though guests are not common at Castle Grundel, Mistress, lost guests comprise the greater portion of those few. I believe that Mr. Shakewit is in conference with his lordship. Shall I take you to them?"

"Yes, kindly do."

"You are close, you two?"

Ekaterina walked slowly in hopes that Ratch would simply lead silently, as she assumed most servants did. She was frustrated on two fronts: She was in fact quite eager to consult with Cyril prior to any encounter with the Poon-Grebe child; and more problematically, Ratch showed no signs of offering her the respectful distant service she imagined commonplace. She willed herself to amble. Ratch strolled. She slowed to a window-shopping pace. Ratch countered with art-gallery languor. Inspired, she risked a pause-for-thought full stop.

Ratch matched her with a second-in-line, please-take-your-time, no-rush-at-all gallantry. Infuriating. Resigned, Ekaterina resumed walking, Ratch still at her side companionably.

"Our acquaintance is of long standing. But, no, I would not say we are close."

"And yet you were quite convincing in your appeal to have him accompany us back to the castle."

"I don't recall that there was convincing required, Ratch. You seemed to have formed a fast friendship with Mr. Shakewit on your own."

"We have mutual interests."

"Yes. As have Mr. Shakewit and I."

"Forgive me, Mistress. For I am very inexperienced in some matters. But I would not have thought that an increasingly notable seer, as yourself, and a tavern entertainer — however outlandish or inspired — would have much in common, at all. Well, save perhaps the venue, itself."

Ekaterina drew to a stop, again. "It takes no notable vision, whatsoever, Ratch, to see that you possess far greater experience than you currently claim. You know what the Jakes & Japes is. You know what it accommodates: ambition, mainly, that tricky quality. Is it the ambition to be recognized for one's gifts, or merely perceived as one who has any? I think, Ratch, that if you believed of me the former rather than the latter, we would not be speaking in this way, now. So, if you have doubts, express them; questions, ask them."

"Mistress, I mean no disrespect and if I may be quite frank with you I have little interest in the integrity of your increasing celebrity, save this: that my lord's interests are served."

"I have been requested by your lord's lady, Ratch. If I am sincere, if I am charlatan, my purposes are still best served by obtaining her satisfaction. Is that not also the satisfaction of your master? Are not their hopes in concert?"

Ratch said nothing for a moment and gazed at Ekaterina contemplatively.

"They may be, Mistress. They may be."

As has been illustrated, Lord Vadney Poon-Grebe had a knack for dungeons. Though not outwardly ferocious, there was within him an ingenious sense for the unsettling effect. Years spent at Castle Grundel no doubt contributed. Vadney's cradle was gothic and grotesque — metaphorically, so far as we know. But there was more to Vadney's ability than a familiarity with overpowering masonry and frustrating frontal approaches. Vadney could arrange the most benign and delicate of architectural elements and/or decorative scenes into something quite sinister with fluid surety: the divan angled thusly, the drape to filter the light like so, only this candle lit, and so on. As a child, his precocious abilities cost the household any number of competent but sensitive domestics. Even his parents, inured as they were to Castle Grundel's proud ugliness, were rattled by Vadney's macabre manipulations of the portable furnishings.

So, it was something of an anomaly when Mistress Ekaterina and Ratch entered the dungeon and felt no dread specific to the room, at all.

Now, this produced no surprise in Ekaterina, as she'd never seen the room before. But Ratch was — another anomaly — quite visibly shaken. Shaken but not perturbed. Shaken by not being perturbed.

This room, which had until very recently, been a chamber of palpably nefarious promise now seemed almost workaday, almost well-intentioned. Papers with hand-quilled notes and diagrams littered the floor; scrolls were attached and unfurled across devices, obscuring the insidious intent plain on their faces. This had been done, Ratch gasped in realization, to provide additional writing surfaces. This artful room, once so exacting in its elegant malevolence was now cluttered and eccentric as any alchemist's lair. It looked studious, busy — gad! — even productive! Worse yet, practical!

Lord Poon-Grebe and Cyril were huddled closely over a document thick with scribbling. They had, evidently, interrupted their conversation only long enough for the marquis to yell, "Enter." They were quite engrossed, flushed and wide-eyed over these mysterious manuscripts.

Ratch and Ekaterina stood, unacknowledged for seconds before the manservant spoke, with a trace of trepidatious emotion in his voice, "My lord?" Vadney and Cyril turned without rising from their hunched positions, as if they had forgotten their own response to the knock on the door as soon as it had been uttered.

"Oh, Ratch! Mistress Blatatat! How are you? We have been having the most illuminating conversation! Mr. Shakewit is really quite astonishingly clever!"

Lord Poon-Grebe rose finally and made a welcoming gesture, inviting Ekaterina farther into the room, though there was no place to sit and, indeed, little room to walk without treading upon some scrap of parchment.

"Are you familiar with his General Eminence & Notoriety Index & Usefulness System?" Vadney turned to Cyril, "Have I got that right?"

Cyril nodded like the proud father at the well-received recital of an unpromising son.

Ekaterina said only, "Passingly."

"Oh, you must get to know it thoroughly!" Vadney bubbled. "It's absolutely marvelous."

"You are too kind, my lord," Cyril said in a tone that Ekaterina, if no one else, could read clearly. Cyril was as vain as he was clever. Too kind? Cyril could certainly operate quite comfortably, unburdened and untroubled by quite a bit more kindness than one compliment in a castle basement delivered before a dubious mystic and manservant.

"Is it, my lord?"

"Oh, beyond measure! You see, it's a system for setting in motion a kind of reputation-building engine. It's sort of legend-development technique. Fascinating!"

"Sir," Ratch cracked. "I'm certain Mr. Shakewit's method is very deserving of study and I'm certain his lordship knows best the appropriate time and habits of such investigation. But the dungeon, my lord . . ."

Lord Vadney glanced quickly, almost indifferently around the cluttered room. "Oh, yes, Ratch. Not to worry. I can have the dungeon back in shape in no time. But that's the very point of Mr. Shakewit's system! For what good is my work . . ."

"Your artistry," Cyril interjected.

"Oh, yes, well, all right, then," he reddened with pleasure. "My artistry. What good is it if no one knows of it?"

"And, I take it, Mr. Shakewit has a plan to help you reach people with your artistry, my lord?"

"He certainly does, Mistress! He certainly does. More than a plan: a comprehensive system for developing a celebrated persona. Look here," Vadney pointed at various papers about him, randomly, it seemed to his audience, while enumerating the elements of Cyril's scheme:

"One: Face Your Name.

Two: Name Your Face.

Three: Find Your Folk.

Four: Fake Your Fate.

Five: Take Your Place."

Cyril prompted, "And Six, your lordship."

"Ah, yes. Six: Watch Your Ass."

Cyril and Vadney looked upon their audience like a stage conjurer and assistant who had pulled in quick succession not only a rabbit, but conjoined rabbit twins, a unicorn grazing on four-leafed clovers and St. Jasper's Badger, itself, from a borrowed top hat. The reception was more muted than they'd hoped.

Ekaterina appeared entirely unimpressed, as if she'd seen the trick before and a version that ended rather more fantastically, at that. Ratch looked — not to be unkind, for anyone who met him knew this to be untrue — merely stupid.

"Of course, these are just chapters, as it were: the broad categories of action and orientation. It's not the plan in its full richness and detail of application," Lord Poon-Grebe said hastily.

"Of course, my lord," Ekaterina said. "It sounds compelling."

"Oh, it is! It is! You see what is meant, here, by Facing Your Name is, as I understand it — and correct me, please, Mr. Shakewit — is one must assess and evaluate one's current, what was it, Reputational Valuation, that is, the 'V Rating' . . ."

Cyril cleared his throat. "My lord, forgive me for interrupting, but while I am most flattered by your enthusiasm and most eager to continue our discussion at your pleasure, Mistress Blatatat has quite serious business of her own to attend to and it has grown quite late."

"Indeed. Indeed, you are right, Mr. Shakewit. Mistress Blatatat, please, know that every resource I have at my own disposal is at yours."

"You are most generous, my lord. And

please know that I will spare no effort, myself, to obtain for your lord- and ladyship the desired result."

"I have no doubt of it. Now, is there anything outstanding that keeps you from sleep? Of what assistance may I be, presently?"

"Sir, I wish only to ask your own insight into your son's condition and for your hopes as to his restoration to his former self."

Lord Poon-Grebe stammered, "Oh, yes . . . I . . . that is . . . we, both . . . even all . . . we hope for my wife's . . . our . . . son to be restored to traveling . . . to full health, full health . . . and to full, of course, that is to say, full, Nelson . . . ness."

Ekaterina waited a moment while Lord Poon-Grebe shifted on his feet, silently. His look of relief when Cyril spoke suggested the sudden removal of an irregularly shaped object from an unaccommodating body part.

"We have covered so much tonight, Lord Poon-Grebe. You have been so giving of your time and attention. I am most appreciative and loath to impose upon you further at such an hour. And, Mistress Blatatat, your time, too, charged as you are with such an important task, is precious. If you are ready to retire and will permit me, I will escort you back to your chamber. We all, no doubt, will need our rest and strength in the upcoming hours."

"I'm surprised Ratch left us to ourselves," Ekaterina said, looking backward over her shoulder. "He's a watchful type."

Cyril laughed easily. "Watchful and a bit possessive, perhaps. I think he needs a moment to check in with his master, who has found, if I may say so, a new friend. Did you see how excited Lord Poon-Grebe was about the G.E.N.I.U.S.?"

"Cyril, you need to be careful about this."

"About this what? A lot of care has gone into the system. You, of all people, know that."

"That's precisely my point, Cyril. I, of all people. And why is that?"

"I don't understand, Tessie."

"Don't call me that, Cyril! Of course, I know the work that went into the system! In great part, I was the work that went into the system! But what do you think people will think if they discover that? What will they conclude if they know that Mistress Ekaterina Blatatat, the mysterious seer, gifted visionary, was the first project of a program devised by a tavern performer in the Sink, of all places, for developing reputation? If they knew that Mistress Ekaterina Blatatat is not in actuality the illegitimate daughter of a minor Vladistanian noble but plain Tessie Trewes of Clambroth Lane, East Pudge, Boyledin, the most recent of innumerable generations of Sink-dwellers, what, Cyril, would they conclude?"

"Tess . . . Ekaterina . . . Mistress Blatatat! I'm sorry. I get it. I understand your concern."

"You don't, Cyril! You don't. You understand a number of things startlingly, disconcertingly well. But you don't understand this. The community I serve are highly superstitious and easily spooked."

"Well, of course, they are! They're bloody credulous idiots! By Jasper's Favorite Nightshirt, we knew that ages ago.

We built your reputation on that very fact, from the first we Found Your Folk! Who else but your folk would buy that you were even a trace Vladistanian? They're flea-wits! You've just looked upon the plan again, Ekaterina. Lord Poon-Grebe seemed to grasp it easily enough — and I'm not too decorous to point out that he may not quite rise to the intellectual level of the standard-issue upper-class blockhead. And I know you now understand it as well as I, myself. So, what's the panic? Now, that we're both standing within grasping range of something very promising."

"Ratch clearly already suspects that I'm a fraud and a huckster."

"But you are not in the employ of Ratch."

"I know that, you clod! I'm in the employ of Lady Camilla Fitz-Victim Poon-Grebe, who, though her credulity is debatable, is surely no idiot . . ."

"A little loud, Mistress."

" . . . and is, additionally, one of the richest, most powerful, mean-spirited and paranoid women of all Maybia . . ."

"Quite loud, actually."

" . . . a woman reported to have fired and sent to the workhouse a scullery maid for presenting a leering reflection in a soup tureen . . ."

"Oh, now, very loud. Quite shouty."

" . . . and testifying in court, personally, against two members of the High Chamber for their lack of character and competence by evidence of their profuse sweatiness!"

"Please, Ekaterina, you are echoing, now."

"Sweatiness, Cyril! If there's a single member of the High Council who weighs less than a . . . a . . . Well, I can't think of an analogy for fatness that doesn't already involve the High Council, but still."

Cyril approached her in a way that was both tender and wary, the way one would a favorite aunt wielding an andiron and dementia. She seemed to him to have exhausted some of her fervor, but caution, he thought not ill advised. He laid his hands on her shoulders, as much to get her attention as to comfort her, for she seemed some distance away.

"We are in the ancestral home of one of, perhaps, the most prestigious family in the history of this country, Tessie."

She reacted, but he raised a finger to her lips before the sound left her lips.

"Yes, Tess. Let me speak to you for a moment as I knew you first and remind you of how far you are from where you've come."

She calmed.

"The system works. It works, in part, because it doesn't matter if people know it's in play or not. I could go to Lady Poon-Grebe now and explain it and, I'm convinced, I could make her see how it only magnifies the pertinent qualities of its subject. It's not trickery. It's not a ruse — or not all the time, anyway. The system helps people talk about their gifts and put them right before the best, most receptive audience."

He paused to catch his breath. He locked eyes with Tessie Trewes, formerly of Clambroth Lane. "It ain't a swindle if the paying customer leaves satisfied. And, Tessie, you're the best. The very best. You have — with only modest help from me — worked up an absolutely sterling routine.

It's just one hell of a show."

Cyril's exhortation, he thought, should have roused his friend, steeled her nerve, focused her vision and, perhaps, inspired an insistence that his own contribution to her increasing eminence was more than, strictly speaking, just "modest." He was surprised, therefore, when at its conclusion she looked more confused and forlorn than before, and possibly more than he could ever recall.

From their first acquaintance as children in the streets of the Sink, Tessie had struck Cyril as (he would never have phrased it thus at the time) a person of moment. At 9, she had purpose; by 11, gravity; by her early teens, when most girls of the Sink had already attached themselves to the habits or husbands who would keep them in the Sink forever, Tessie was aloof. In moments of self-awareness and candor, for Cyril did have those, he recognized that much as Tessie was the beneficiary of his scheme, she was also its origin. Something about her, everything about her, suggested to him that a person need not be bound by time, place or circumstance of birth, by early shabbiness or inexperience. These were local conditions. Why should one accept them as fixed, when one could clearly see in Tessie Trewes, for example, the will, the drive, the unshakeable conviction of the possibility of change?

And, yet, here she was now, shaken and unconvinced. Miles from the Sink and a far greater, immeasurable, distance from the gritty, grimy, gross details of their early lives, in a castle through which the very sap of the nation's history coursed, Ekaterina was again Tessie Trewes of the slums of Boyledin.

She spoke softly. "It's not a swindle, at all, Cyril. It's not a routine. It's not a show."

She paused, but he knew not to speak.

"I think I might be magic."

Mornings at the Castle Grundel were, as a rule, challenging. Or to speak more precisely, mornings at Castle Grundel were, as a rule, a series of overlapping, interlocking, competing, clashing challenges to rival the feats of athleticism and endurance of the combatants in the quadrennial displays on the ancient game fields at Dent-on-Viscera.

The mundane needs and expectations of the lord and lady of the house were more often than not diametrically and aggressively opposed. So, imagine half a circle actively hating its other half and pursuing it endlessly, while the other half dedicates itself to resentful evasion. Mornings at Castle Grundel were, as a rule, an ouroboros of marital acrimony. This was a peculiar morning.

Mistress Blatatat was implacable, inscrutable, again. But she was alone in her composure. She sat, still and seemingly serene in an ornately upholstered wingback in one of innumerable reading-, sitting-, drawing-, musing-, fiddling-, stalling-, fretting rooms of the home. She might have been calmly, even light-heartedly wondering about that very architectural segmentation of the functions of daily emotional and intellectual life and the stilted rigidity it may contribute to Maybia's aristocrats. But, then, she might not have.

Across from her on a similar chair, the Marchioness Poon-Grebe sat bolt upright, twitching intensely by minute degrees, like a neurasthenic dowsing wand. She was not speaking. Her thin lips were, in fact, drawn tight as a Boyledin widow's purse, but one imagines the more aurally acute fauna within miles of Castle Grundel shivering at the pitch of Lady Poon-Grebe's nervous thrum.

The lord of the manor was draped somewhat more sloppily across a plush divan, a not-unusual posture. He was, however, if logy, fully conscious, faintly smiling and apparently at ease in the presence of his wife — the last of which, especially, would on any other morning be quite remarkable.

On this morning even Ratch, so expertly attuned to the phases and forms of his master's many moods, was distracted by the drama of this new context. Customarily, he stood inside the door nearest Lord Poon-

Grebe, but his habitual poise was belied by furtive eyes, which flitted across the others in the room as if confronting an important message in a foreign grammar. And to look upon Mr. Cyril Shakewit was to stoutly gird Ratch's incomprehension.

Cyril looked, himself, like a breakaway element of an exotic alphabet: a shard from an ancient cypher chiseled in pockmarked stone; a recalcitrant figure inked on frayed papyrus. His posture was unnaturally angled; he clashed with his chair in contentious geometry. His expression was even more puzzling, containing as it did a multitude of aspects engaged in a hard-fought battle for his face. Shock and incredulity buffeted each other on the low ridge of his lips, while his eyebrows were claimed then lost then regained by confusion, skepticism and awe, respectively.

His cheeks puffed, slackened and sank in turn, and wonder, worry and trepidation sent troops across those plains, where they skirmished fiercely. His forehead contorted and rippled like a shallow sea churned by warships at close quarters. Taken as a whole, Cyril's face was mobile map of combat, an animated encyclopedia of conflict.

But in Cyril's eyes there was an opportunistic gleam. In the midst of these warring forces there were bright mercenaries who would, the shine covertly boasted, seize chance and find profit whichever grand faction triumphed.

"You are well rested, I hope, Mistress Blatatat," Lady Poon-Grebe managed to squeak past her lips.

"Thank you, Lady Poon-Grebe. I am."

"I am glad. I pray that you will not find

my eagerness for you to begin your ... process ... impatient or uncivil. Please be assured that I abide by your counsel and trust your methods implicitly. If there are preparations that must be made or practice that must be observed I shall not question or interfere. But, to be quite direct, Mistress Blatatat, I am quite beside myself and fraught with concern for my darling son."

"Your concern for your son is understandable, and no less noble than one would expect of your ladyship. I promise you that I shall make no unnecessary delays."

Cyril's eyes quickened and flickered and honed in on Ekaterina's face. But if he had made the eye contact he sought he could not tell.

"Though I must caution your ladyship, that at this point, I cannot foretell the specific means or methods we must undertake, nor the duration of our undertaking. For, every human spirit is vast and labyrinthine; and from what you told me of your Nelson's fineness and richness, his may be a most intricate soul."

At this, both Lady Poon-Grebe and Cyril nodded, though the latter more slightly and the former without the barely noticeable smile of relief and satisfaction.

Ekaterina continued: "And pardon me, please, for speaking directly, as well, Lady Poon-Grebe, for this may be hard on your ears. But for the scion of such an illustrious lineage as your own and the ward and beneficiary of one such as your husband's to have succumbed as he has suggests a great, malicious will and intent."

Lady Poon-Grebe was stopped mid-eye roll at the mention of the Poon-Grebe legacy by this dire pronouncement. She gasped thinly: "I was afraid."

"We can accomplish much, I am hopeful," Ekaterina said, softly. "But we must be prepared for a pitched and perhaps lengthy effort."

Lady Camilla's sharp, wan face set resolutely — which was to stack resoluteness upon resoluteness, as if stone suddenly made up its mind. "Whatever is necessary, Mistress Blatatat. Whatever you need, for however long. Just restore my boy to me."

At once, the rival nations on Cyril's face declared a global truce and whole populations celebrated in a beaming *pax universalis*. His eyes glittered like freshly minted high-denomination coins.

Lord Poon-Grebe roused slightly, to query weakly, "Yes, of course, however long. But that's 'long' as in, say, 'that was quite a long yawn,' rather than, say, 'that was quite a long sermon', or 'my, what a long visit from relatives,' yes?"

At a glance from Lady Poon-Grebe, Vadney did his best to dissolve into a fine, light mist on the divan.

"You are anxious, of course, Lady Poon-Grebe, Lord Poon-Grebe, to have your son well, and I have now just given you reason to feel all the more so — though I know you shall not shy from challenge on your son's behalf. Still, I have been direct and perhaps grim. I pray this next will offer relief: With your permission, I would like to begin. My lady, may I be introduced to Nelson?"

Nelson Poon-Grebe's bedchamber was vast. This was, given its location in the seemingly endless number of vast spaces in the interior of Castle Grundel, unsurprising. What was less predictable was its cheerful opulence. The room was a riot of color and texture and fabric and ornament. Furniture of different eras and lands was arranged in mixed clusters creating the illusion of many different rooms within the one; paintings of all recognizable domestic schools were interspersed with great idols of primitive practices; classical statuary shared space with vases of colorful and common flowering weeds; shelves lined with tall volumes bound in sumptuous leather were bookended with devices comprised of gears, lenses and ratcheting levers so intricate that one could not confidently proclaim them coincidentally beautiful utensils or fortuitously functional objets d'art.

There were numerous lamps, candles and

candelabra about the room; at night, it must appear the very vault of heaven. None were lit at this early hour, though, and none were needed. Morning light was softly pouring, like a rich and delicate sauce, in through the many panes of the leaded glass windows — which must have been crafted with some honeyed element to filter light, remove its impurities and leave only the most stimulating solar gold.

The effect of stepping into Nelson's room from the connecting stairway, for his chamber was immediately under the peak of the castle's highest turret, was like discovering an entire exotic bazaar held hostage by a demented wizard with exquisite taste.

The bed itself was at first difficult to discern — or difficult to discern as a bed, per se. Nelson lay atop a low hill of pillows and pelts in an outcropping of the turret, directly in the path of the strengthening light.

If Nelson's room was a bazaar, however magically transported, the boy himself seemed its most-prized offering. Elevated, illuminated, the pale, soft-skinned dumpling of a boy looked like a sacrificial cherub in effigy, a votive in smooth white lard.

A quintet of divergent concern gazed upon this monument in morning light, their unvoiced thoughts pell-mell with individual and variant interest.

Lady Poon-Grebe managed to imbue her rigid posture with a palpable sense of hurtling motion, like the stiff wooden figurehead of the fleetest freighter. Buffeted by swells, sea-spray and the cutting wind of a ship at speed, she radiated maternity like cultists do confidence. Her mission was simple, uncomplicated, inarguable: her son.

    Lord Poon-Grebe's air was quite different. On the very few occasions he had previously been coaxed, cajoled or compelled to enter his step-son's garish lair (for so he found it: its luxury striking him as faintly perfumed, indolent and, if he had to put a word to it, feminine) his distaste had been evident. This unease was nowhere to be found in his expression today, however. Where previously he shifted uncomfortably from foot to foot, rolled his eyes from artifact to urn to avoid settling too long on any one, he now twitched and scanned with a very different energy. He looked markedly like an inconsistently continent puppy. The prospect of a successful outcome, the mere possibility of the de facto separation of himself from his wife was so delightful to him that his own thoughts, too, centered on that same subject: her son.

Cyril's thoughts were, no one could be surprised, more free ranging, though certainly they touched upon the young noble. But whereas the lord and lady of the castle both entertained a linear vision of rejuvenation and removal, Cyril's thoughts progressed in mad spirals of possibility. He conjured dramatic tableau, swapped roles, playing them out as tragedy, comedy, farce, folly, in turn. He tested them for heroic and/or profitable story lines starring a quick-witted escapee from the streets of the Sink, who intended never to go back without rousing fanfare sufficient to wound the pride of every thunder god in the world's pantheon.

Mistress Ekaterina Blatatat, for all the weird and witchy trappings of her profession, had maintained a seriousness of mind common to the (few) sober women of the Sink. These women were sharp and skeptical and practical in the extreme. They led anti-poetic lives (those with the ill luck to have married poets, most especially) and had resolutely anti-poetic frames of mind. Flights of fancy were no more likely for these women than flights of swine. Paradoxically, it was this very air of grim presence that elevated Ekaterina in her practice. She provided a stable contact with the here-and-now while simultaneously promising contact with the beyond-and-always. She was an anchor in the ether.

But Ekaterina's own thoughts in this very particular here-and-now had become unmoored. In fact, her thoughts had never been more existential or arcane. In all of her previous performances, Ekaterina had been confident, observant, almost removed. She read her clients and her audiences as easily as she could a child's primer. The wisdom she gave to them, they first and unfailingly gave to her: the widows and their needs to to be loved still from the far side of death (the young ones with permission, too, to be loved again this side); the grieving parents' desperate desires to be absolved for having outlived their children, who became wise, content and forgiving in their heavenly (always heavenly) homes; the orphaned at any age, hollowed by loneliness, which only could be soothed by the promise of parents become now omnipresent and approving, and so on, and so on.

If it was not easy, it was simple. Or had been, at first and for quite a while. Long enough to build a reputation that reached outside the confines of the Sink, beyond the limits of Boyledin, across the Poon itself to the Continent. Far enough at any rate to have entered channels wending eventually to Lady Camilla Fitz-Victim Poon-Grebe and bringing Ekaterina here.

But recently the process had become unsimple. It had become complicated. It had become mysterious to the one person for whom it had never been so — to Ekaterina herself. Into the orderly routine of her practice had slipped strange information.

While comforting a young and willowy widow whose prettiness was only heightened by her grief, tears like dew on the flora of her long lashes, Ekaterina shuddered. As certainly as she knew this lovely, mournful, soft-spoken wife sat before her, she knew the presumed deceased was at that very moment quaffing rum in great quantities in the company of several profoundly ample and voluble women, matching him mug for mug, in the far northern city of Guernsey-on-Tipple. (Ekaterina also knew in that moment, surely as one emerges from water wet, that the man had never for a fleeting instant been happier in his life.)

And once, seated across from a finely dressed and quite young gentleman of evident means (one of those fellows before whom the world seems to contort to fulfill their great expectations of it) Ekaterina saw a surprising truth clear as the burnished buttons on his overcoat of Flenish wool: This young man's benefactor was no lost aristocratic relative but a recent escapee from Blackthorne Prison, whom the lad had once unwittingly assisted in the crime that led to his incarceration. The youngster had in fact not only pointed out the manse of the town's wealthiest resident, the departing carriage transporting the homeowner to a two-week hunting trip in the Gnarls, but also the most sheltered entrance into the stately home, itself, and the widely known location of the affluent man's wall safe. (It must be noted that the boy's early low expectations, now artificially inflated, were quite directly tied to his startling and still-pure stupidity.)

The frequency of the insights had steadily increased. Ekaterina had applied her Sink-strong will and learned to, if not ignore, compartmentalize them, so as to still deliver her customer-pleasing product. She comforted herself that she would be able to do so indefinitely. But, as if the visions themselves had found some doltish village boy to show the safest route to pillage the luxury of her lobes, her defenses were circumvented.

"What do you mean by that, Mistress Blatatat?" she would hear just after she shared. Now no longer only trance*like,* the words came to her from whence she knew not.

"It is not for me to assign meaning," she would counter. "I have looked where the spirits and signs that travel with you have directed. So, what does it mean to you?"

"It's about my mother, isn't it?"

"Sure."

Ekaterina's clientele being what it was and their faculties being what they were, there was little outcry. In fact, she found that this new wrinkle, this redirection, increased return business. She extended engagements and still left clamoring clients waiting, pleading with her to return (this, Cyril assured her, was much to be desired: "Create a new appetite in others and you will never be hungry yourself," he said in his oft-impenetrably-aphoristic manner).

    Business did not suffer, but Ekaterina fretted. Cyril was comfortable with weird; Ekaterina believed in will. Cyril saw opportunity in eccentricity and unpredictability; Ekaterina put stock in grit and endurance. She possessed and cultivated these in herself. Now, she felt infiltrated, and she was afraid. For the first time in a very long time, she was afraid — that the world was fundamentally other than she had thought. She wondered what she had put herself next to: "Fake your own fate, indeed," she thought half mournfully, half acidly, wondering if she could still blame everything on Cyril.

    Ekaterina's habits of professionalism were anchored in an autonomous part of her brain by now, though, a region not hospitable to such philosophical turmoil. She stepped toward Nelson's cushiony bier, head bowed slightly and cocked to the side as if listening to some faint call from deep in the castle. She stopped just short of its outermost fringe, pivoting to pace its forward arc to the right, following the wall of the room all the way round to the point where she began. Her pace throughout was slow, steady and deliberate but at moments slight tremors animated her hands and fingers. Here, she seemed to be fanning flames; there, she seemed to be performing some musical number on an invisible, exotic instrument. But she never spoke nor made any other indication of the purpose or progress of this survey.

 Once returned to the edge of the bed, she turned back to the boy-bearing mound and laced her fingers together over her belly.

John Rodat

She stood in that way for long silent minutes. The light streaming in through the window coursed around her, reducing her to silhouette and casting a shadow like an accusing finger at the three other adults, two of whom stood their ground (Vadney shifted slightly leftward). The level of repressed manic anticipation in the sensuous ornateness of the room gave it the air of the stand-by line for the last show at a Boyledin Burlesque, and when Ekaterina dropped her hands to her sides and strode out the door to the hallway, the simultaneous confusion and relief in the room was miasmic. Lord and Lady Poon-Grebe and Cyril had been let off the very hook on which all their hopes were suspended. They followed her, trailing waves of mingled emotion as tangled and riotous as the patterns in the B'zerki carpets scattered about the room.

Into the hallway, then down the great winding staircase, through galleries and passageways and rooms quite comfortable and well-suited to conference, thought Cyril and Vadney independently. But as Ekaterina walked on, so did they, obediently.

Cyril soon noticed that they were retracing the very steps which had first brought Ekaterina and himself into the personal presence of Lord and Lady Poon-Grebe, back through the kitchens and pantries and larders. Back to the overwhelming ebony hallway like a frightful night at sea. Back to and through the enormous jaws of the servants' entrance. Cyril thought unpleasantly to himself that they were, after whatever it was that had just happened in Nelson's room, being very slowly, very deliberately regurgitated out of Castle Grundel. The fact he quite ardently hoped to be ingested again worried him in a vague and irritating way. One presumes both Lord and Lady Poon-Grebe recognized sooner than Cyril the route. While neither were victim to Cyril's emetic vision, neither were they at ease. Camilla felt the increasing distance, the retreat from her son as acutely as she did the proximity of the astonished downstairs help, some of whom had never before beheld her and had come to believe she was an invention of more senior staff to keep them alert and active. Vadney had no such qualms and, in fact, rather liked the domestic bustle of the more industrious areas of the castle; but the affinity may well have had something to do with his wife's scarcity in these realms. His current duckling-like position behind her made him glum and thirsty. At each turn taken before reaching the heavy outer doors, he hoped for a merciful diversion through the cellar where he might surreptitiously, if not fully restore his cheer at least fortify himself to withstand this terrible marital company. But when they passed through those doors and into the open courtyard, Vadney winced against the bright light and resigned himself to an extension of this cruel sobriety. To steady himself, he tried to reckon the miles between Castle Grundel and the Sebastian Academy for Curious Boys. Unconsciously, he smacked his lips.

Ekaterina had come to a full halt. The trailing trio followed suit and stood gazing at her back in bewilderment.

She turned to them. The brightness of the open courtyard reflected off her pale face, nearly obliterating her features. For a moment, she appeared just an embodied pair of staring eyes. Without the customary contextualization of lips and brows the eyes were impossible to interpret. They had witnessed, but what?

If Ekaterina had waited one moment longer to speak it is possible one of her companions might have screamed to break the silence or bashed him or herself in the face with a courtyard rock just to feel some agency in the excruciating uncertainty.

"This will be difficult." Though Ekaterina's pronouncement was dire, her listeners all eased visibly at the return to standard modes of earthly communication. So relieved were they at this restoration that they embraced it with avid overlapping babble.

"Oh, Nelson, my Nelson . . ."

"Difficult meaning difficult, or difficult meaning dangerous, or difficult meaning . . ."

"But not terribly slow, I pray . . ."

Ekaterina let them chatter out their nervous release and stood before them calm and composed. The clouds drifted leisurely above, sifting and softening the sun. Her face no longer bleached and inhuman, she had resumed her typical mien: that of resolute competence. If there had been traces of amazement in those eyes, a delicate filigree of fear, there was no evidence that lingered.

"Yes, difficult. Something — some thing — has coalesced around your son, Lady Poon-Grebe. I cannot as yet determine if Nelson is merely in it or wholly of it. And intention — if there is intention and not just incident or accident — is unclear. These things, I must determine first before I can remedy."

"But is he . . . will he . . . ?" Lady Poon-Grebe's voice was so strained with emotion that it might fairly be described as piteous — a quality that no living soul ever had ascribed to her before. Even Vadney felt an unfamiliar twinge, though he found it easier to think "missed breakfast" than the patently preposterous "spousal sympathy."

"While there is much yet to discover, Lady Poon-Grebe, I can comfort you that, at the moment, Nelson is bodily sound. He is, on this plane, still vital. Please forgive the blunt language, my lady, but I seek only to assuage those fears I may: Nelson is not dying."

Lady Poon-Grebe hitched and bit off a gasp of sweet air like the first morsel after a long fast.

"But he's not exactly lively, is he?" The women hardly had time to turn their meaningful, menacing eyes toward Cyril before Vadney spoke, as well, demanding a quick pivot.

"And he's certainly not motivated."

"Nelson is beset," Ekaterina said. "It will require a great effort to uncover the cause and determine the most efficacious action."

She surprised herself by continuing to speak.

"But I believe that I can help him."

Vadney and Cyril sat sipping the finest — not to mention the earliest (breakfast wine, who knew?) — intoxicant Cyril had ever tasted. Lady Poon-Grebe and Mistress Blatatat had removed themselves to discuss some details of the effort to help Nelson and the men received the very clear message that their input was at this time most uncompromisingly unwished for. Cyril was not particularly pleased with the exile, comfortable though it was.

"It's not as if we meant to hold their hands or read over their shoulders, or something," he groused. "I don't see why we shouldn't be involved."

Lord Poon-Grebe assented. "It was rather a slap in the face, wasn't it? Mind you, I'm usually quite content, more than, to allow Lady Poon-Grebe all the privacy she might desire. I'm not one of those clingy types, you know. Quite the opposite, really. Mystifies me to see those husbands and wives who just can't seem to function without the other. They put me in mind of those side-by-side monstrosities from Admiral Cork's Travelogues, joined at the hip."

A shiver ran through Vadney at the thought.

"It is obvious that your lord- and ladyship are both admirably independent people. There is no question."

"Well, yes. Thank you for noticing. It's just the most natural conduct, I believe. Men and women being what they are — and Camilla, in particular, being what she is. It is only sensible that there be a . . ."

"An appropriate proportionality?"

"Oh, yes! Well said! 'An appropriate proportionality' in their common and their private spheres. And yet, some husbands seem to lack a sense for this balance, altogether. Do you know Lord Chutney Mantiss, the Earl of Hertz-Nuptial?"

Vadney seemed to have forgotten that his immaculately and tastefully attired companion was a commoner in borrowed finery — Vadney's own. Cyril though was keenly aware of the absent-minded inclusiveness and familiarity. If it were not likely to derail the conversation and the fellow feeling, Cyril might very well have stood, bowed and thrown the first flower he could pick to the first beautiful maiden he could spy in the first convenient crowd of cheering townsfolk. Instead, he said, "By reputation, only."

"Oh, well, then you must have heard: The lunatic tried to bring his wife to the Misplaced Rake's Club!"

"He didn't."

"He did! Flabbergasting. She wasn't admitted, of course. Thankfully. But what could he have been thinking? Caused an incredible sensation. The papers are still prattling on about exclusive practices and whatnot. Awful headache for the club."

"You are a member of the club, Lord Poon-Grebe?"

"Oh, yes. For ages. Forever, really. There's been a Poon-Grebe in the Rake from its very beginning."

"And Lord Mantiss? Is he a member of long standing?"

Vadney pondered, taking a long sip of his excellent wine. "Well, no, now that you mention it. He's really rather newish. Frankly, I don't know how he got in."

"And has he been much involved in the club activities since his acceptance?"

"Fortunately, no. Strange. He was very keen to get in. Or so I hear. I don't much participate in the administrative stuff. Wonder if maybe I should. The admission policy has certainly gone slack. Mantiss is a terrible drip."

Vadney looked around the room

conspiratorially. "Don't say so to my wife, though. She's friendly with that madwoman wife of his. Anyway, it's odd. Campaign to get into a club and then participate in only such a way as to irritate. Aside from the aforementioned scandal, I don't think I've ever seen Mantiss at the club. It is possible we just keep different schedules, I suppose. But he has been notably absent at even those events that traditionally draw the full ambulatory membership. Often the semi-ambulatory, as well. I know that he was not in attendance for the Fancy-Dress Regatta, the Donkey Auction nor even the Rite of Harald's Hallowed Hamper!"

"It is curious, my lord. I wonder if Lord Mantiss pursued membership for reasons other than fraternal frolic."

"Really? Why would he do such thing? Why petition to join a club in whose activities you disdain to participate?"

"His reasons may not have been wholly his own, my lord. Can you tell me more about Lady Mantiss?"

"Oh, she's one of those terrible, strident do-gooder types. Always meddling in civic or social affairs, ranting about this or that unfair something or other, or on behalf of this or that sorry someone or other. For a while she was trying to solicit donations for rooftop wash stations for chimney sweeps, to prevent them from walking the streets sooty between jobs. Said they were unsightly. After that she commissioned some inkpot to write a melodramatic serial about the dangers of musical ensembles. *The Sinful Sorry Saga & Expected Egregious End of Piccolo Promiscuous*, it was called. Then it was, I believe, an attempt to change the name of the Boyledin Tower timepiece."

"The Big Black Clock?"

"The same. Weird, that one."

"Quite. Now, is Lord Mantiss supportive of her crusades?"

"Indubitably. He is her foremost and often sole follower. For all the good it does either. There's not a noble in Maybia who doesn't regard her as anything less than a complete crackpot — save my wife — and him a dutiful pet."

"Interesting. So, among their peers Lord and Lady Mantiss are viewed askance and taken unseriously."

"Unseriously in the extreme, I'd say."

"And none of Lady Mantiss's causes have gained ground or popular support?"

"None. Well, none that is . . ."

"Not till the fracas at the Misplaced Rake?"

"Yes. I suppose that's so. This one has

rather caught fire."

"Delightful!"

Vadney's face puckered. "Is it?"

"A nuisance, certainly, Lord Poon-Grebe. And a difficult one to countenance, directed as it is at such a venerable organization — nay, institution — as the Misplaced Rake's Club. But there is a fascinating aspect to this, one that may be useful to you, as it fits quite precisely into what I hope I am not too presumptuous to regard as our plan. Fracas — to use your word — is very much a part of my G.E.N.I.U.S. Do you happen to recall which papers had men at the club when Lady Mantiss made her attempt?"

"Oh, it was a great horrid lot."

In recent years, Maybia had experienced a sudden fecundity of publishing. The slow progression of literacy from the nation's cloistered ecclesiastics to the increasingly less-rare sensitive and/or scholarly nobility had infected the folk. Now, in addition to hymnals, hagiographies and histories, along with essays, adventures and terrible verse, there were novels, novellas, dailies, weeklies, monthlies, chronicles, reviews, treatises, analyses, broadsides, diatribes, pamphlets, leaflets, journals of opinion and, most terrifyingly of all, that novelty of unexamined occurrence known as "news."

Cyril began listing just some of those "news" papers now available — unavoidable — in the streets of Boyledin, in roughly descending order of ethics and roughly ascending order of popularity: *The Whale Street Journal*, *The Boyledin Best Intelligencer*, *Maybia Today* . . ."

"I don't pay very close attention to these things, I'm afraid, Cyril. I've no idea why any one much cares about what happened to someone else, somewhere else, just this morning."

"*The Town Tattler, Ramsey's Miscellany* . . ."

"You know, young Lord Barnaby Grab has written satirical essays for, what's it called, *The Constant Comment*, I believe."

"*The Ocular* . . ."

"But Barney does love the company of his own opinion."

"*The Fervid Inquisitor* . . ."

"Oh, hey!"

Cyril ceased his drone.

"That last. That sounds familiar. There was a fellow lingering about the club. I mistook him for the new doorman. Tipped him rather too generously, I now realize. I think he said that, that *Turgid Whatsit*."

"*Fervid Inquisitor?*"

"Yes. Certainly. Could be. Something

quite like that."

"Short man? Notable mustache?"

"Yes! Really a very forward kind of facial adornment. Quite impertinent, in fact! Do you know him?"

"We are acquainted."

"Well, what a coincidence. I thought we must know some of the same people, of course, Boyledin being what it is. But I wouldn't have guessed . . ."

"Have you spoken with him, Lord Poon-Grebe?"

"Spoken with him? I suppose I must have done when I gave him that wad of yelps. Something casually magnanimous-y, I imagine: 'You really have the knack of doors,' or, 'Here, buy yourself a thing that appeals to doormen,' or something. I really gave him several opportunities to correct my misapprehension, you know."

"Of course, my lord. Some people will take advantage. But did you speak to him about Lord and Lady Mantiss?"

"No, not at all."

"Has anyone at the club made a statement?"

"Why, yes. We're making statements all the time. It's a sociable place, kind of the whole point. Statements, polite questions, warm greetings, bon mots, drink orders, all that sort of thing."

"I'm sorry, my lord. I am being unclear. Has any member or representative of the club formally answered or addressed to the writers a statement regarding the club's policies in respect to the refusal of Lady Mantiss?"

"Why, no! I believe the idea of standing about on the street chattering with that crowd of scruffy scribblers and mad mustaches would be quite unappealing to all members. Except for Barney — that goes without saying — but even he . . ."

"Excellent! My lord, do you have paper and a stylus? We have a correspondence to compose."

Ekaterina sat at the vanity in the room that Lady Poon-Grebe had made clear was hers for however long she needed. She was, the noblewoman said earnestly, to regard the castle and all that it contained — stores, staff, the very stone, itself, should it come to that — as utterly available to her discretionary disposal.

She had not dressed for bed and was still in the striking and austere garment provided for her that morning. She sat gazing at her bare face. As befit an experienced confidence artist, she had become fluent in the unspoken vernacular of physical expression. She was as attuned to the minute twist of a lip, the shiver of a lid, the bloom of a pupil, as an expert swordsman to a clumsy feint. She trained her discernment on the oval glass. The woman within its vine-scrolled frame was, Ekaterina could not deny, weary and afraid. She peered harder and the woman shuddered — a motion unnoticeable to an eye less acute than hers. She stared even harder. She would not let this exterior of exhaustion and dread spur some wincing pity. She pushed deeper, determined to drive on through every soft, yielding weak thing till she found some resistance, something fortified, durable, defiant. She did.

Something simpler and more essential than Lady Poon-Grebe's borrowed smock;

something resolute as Castle Grundel. The reflected lips were set, no slack; the eyes shone, unblinking; four pupils met, none shrank nor startled. She was still tired but she was unafraid.

The day had been long. The first encounter with Nelson Poon-Grebe alone took much out of her. Performances were depleting as a rule, but this had been different. Ekaterina's shows required deep immersed attentiveness and ready spontaneity. It required a kind of cognitive juggling act between those functions of mind: both deep and fleet. And, of course, an ever-present and deliberate theatricality, the striving for effect. But the very act of exertion was fulfilling, thrilling. The effect produced, she was buoyed, elated. And, yes, paid. But today in Nelson's room she had felt exposed and vulnerable in a new way.

She felt that she was being watched.

Which, of course, she was: by Lady Poon-Grebe, Lord Poon-Grebe, Cyril — and very possibly by Nelson himself. This wouldn't have, shouldn't have, didn't bother her in the least. She performed for audiences. It was what she did. But she had, nonetheless, been unnerved. The word "haunted" came to mind. And though she had been quite conscious of the dramatic notes of her exit from the chamber and made sure to strike them clearly, it was an ominous song seemingly already written in her heart, the tune of which echoed through the rest of the day spent with Lady Poon-Grebe.

They patrolled the castle together, performing what Ekaterina referred to as a "spiritual sounding" of the environment in which Nelson had been afflicted. Ekaterina pressed, caressed, fingered, fondled, traced and touched her way through the entire castle. She shivered, shuddered, sighed, muttered darkly and nodded knowingly. The mileage alone should inspire a heavy slumber but Ekaterina was not restful. For she had felt, quite clearly, the presence of another, or others, in the spaces defined by Castle Grundel's beastly building stuffs.

She glanced again at the glass. The eyes that met hers said, "So, you felt it, too, huh?"

She said back, "Damn." Then turned to the sudden rapping at the door.

"Ekaterina! Ekaterina, open up! It's Cyril. C'mon, it's important!"

Cyril was excited. Cyril's excitement, Ekaterina knew, had a peculiarly disruptive power. She rose and opened the door. Cyril tumbled in, flailing finery, as if a Shuhn

Tisian silk merchant had taken to advertising his wares by firing his most elegantly attired dress dummy at customers one limb at a time.

"Opportunity upon opportunity, Ekaterina! This is going to work for everyone! Oh, connections and coincidence, eh? The Jake & Japes is truly a magnificent institution. I knew I wasn't wasting my time. I'm not saying, 'I told you so,' mind you. I certainly had no expectation that chance would present itself with such preposterous facial hair."

"Cyril, I wonder if given the circumstances you could find a way, for me, as a favor, to be slightly less weird. I'm really up to here with weird, presently."

"What? Oh, yes. Right. Sorry. But, well, I've just stumbled on this powder keg."

"Something volatile and destructive?

Apt."

"No, no. Honestly, this is something momentous. Something that could make for . . . Well, I don't know precisely, just yet. But I'll get there. And you, too! This will be great for both of us."

"Cyril, you may have noticed that I've really got actually quite a lot going on just now, as it is. I'm not entirely sure I can weather anything more momentous than the present moment."

"I know, I know. But it's all of a piece. Quite amazingly compact and tidy."

Nothing in Ekaterina's experience of Cyril — from their very first school-room meeting (which had ended with the evacuation of said schoolroom of all the children, a plainly terrorized maiden teacher, some six dozen feral cats and Cyril carrying a satchel of miniature circus costumes and tiny bicycles) to his most recent colorful entrance — allowed for an easy acceptance of the adjectives "compact" or "tidy."

"I just need the tiniest bit of help from you," he said, sweetly.

"No."

"But you haven't every heard . . ."

"It's safer that way."

"But, look . . ."

"No. I don't want to look. I don't want to hear. I don't want to help. I can't afford to help. The redress of possession by some spectral body — or bodies, more likely, there is a lot going on in there — of the youngest member of the most eminent family in Maybia, that's my job. This despite the fact that until very recently, as you well know, I was a swindler. Because, lo and behold, apparently if you play around at the edge of the earthly and the ethereal long enough, if you pester the spirit world persistently, knocking on their doors at all hours of the night then hiding in the hedgerows, they will come and find you!"

"I don't understand. How is that a bad thing?"

"How is it . . . ?"

For a moment the two just looked at each other in expectant confusion. If someone were to look in upon them they might think Cyril and Ekaterina had just been playing game of Sorcerer Says and the Sorcerer had stepped out for a break without calling the next move. (They very quickly would have assumed Cyril the victor, as, clearly, no one had commanded "Call out in exasperation.")

"It's a very bad thing, Cyril!"

It suddenly dawned on Cyril that Ekaterina was extremely fretful, well beyond the usual level he inspired in her. He looked at her with authentic care, sat on the low plush bench at the foot of the bed. He spoke calmly.

"Okay, you're feeling some pressure. I see that. That's completely reasonable. You're right: This is a big deal. The Poon-Grebes. Castle Grundel. History, and whatnot. We are way out of our element."

Cyril paused and looked intently at Ekaterina. Her face was set in a combative resistance, but to Cyril, it looked vulnerable. He spoke softly.

"But, Ekaterina," he gently, gently emphasized the name. "That was the whole point."

Her face shifted and flickered. She tried several expressions in turn, her features not quite working in concert. The effect was of novel and contradictory emotions: amused alarm, indignant acceptance, ferocious fondness.

"Yes, I suppose it was."

Cyril, most unusually, said nothing and just smiled a very small smile. Somehow that tiny twitch of his lips contained nearly the full range of his friend's more dynamic expressive display.

"So, Cyril, what's the plan?"

He shot up like the winner at a parish raffle. "Oh, you're going to love this!"

He paused, mid-pace, turned and faced Ekaterina again. "Well, actually, no. You probably won't. Not right away. But, I assure you, it's brilliant."

Ekaterina made a motion with her hands that was at the exact mid-point between "Please, do come in. It's been so long!" and "My final words are only this: Do your worst." In any event, Cyril took the invitation.

"All right, so, with some minor ambiguities, things are going quite swimmingly for us here, I think."

Ekaterina's eyebrows had resumed their accustomed partnership and sent a single message with clarity.

"Yes, yes, I know. There are details. But that's excellent. That's perfect. We need those details. We're shaking them loose. That's exactly what's supposed to happen at this stage. We've been Faking our Fate, Ekaterina — and thank you very much for letting Lady Poon-Grebe know we might be here a while. Sometimes the fake needs some space. But that's Stage Four. Stage Four!"

"And that's good, why?"

"Oh, come on! Because Five is next! Five!"

"Oh, by Madge's Mittens, Cyril."

"Take Your Place! Five is Take Your Place! We're right at the cusp. We're ready to blow up."

"You mentioned a powder keg. You know that most sane people dread the possibility of explosion. It's almost an instinct for some. And my understanding is that even those more open to the risk find the experience, itself, extremely unpleasant."

"We are at Castle Grundel, Ekaterina. We are not among the sane. We are here, as you said, to retrieve the so and so of such and such from the spectral blah blah blah. I've spent hours, hours, Ekaterina, dressed like drunk nobility discussing the optimal arrangement of torture devices — with drunk nobility! I can now express an informed opinion on both the aesthetic of oppression and effective dungeon drainage. Sane? My school friend is about to become the most celebrated spiritualist in all of the land, of history, of ever, and it's due to the fact that, while also a gifted performer and one of the sharpest and steeliest hustlers to ever scam the Sink, she's also actually, evidently, demonstrably magic! Sane?! Sane is gone, Ekaterina. Forget sane. We're going to be famous."

"A journalist, in the castle? That's preposterous."

Lady Poon-Grebe looked at the faces around the room, growing ever more perplexed that they did not display the full and total agreement that her self-evident exclamation deserved.

"I thought so, as well, I have to admit, until Cyril brought me around" said Vadney, his agreement hoisting Camilla's brow precariously. "But now the others, as well? If you say they're necessary, Mistress Blatatat, well, I suppose you know your business. Though the prospect of the having those Puissian loons, Lord and Lady Sauvignon, here, is bad enough, and the inclusion of the Mantisses is just brain bending."

"Who is this man, this journalist," Lady Poon-Grebe twisted the word into something serrated.

"Sludge. J. Mitchell Sludge," Cyril said, helpfully.

"Admitted to Castle Grundel. It's outrageous, it's ludicrous, it's ridiculous, it's . . ."

"It's G.E.N.I.U.S.," Cyril said, softly enough to be heard only by Lord Poon-Grebe, himself.

Ekaterina joined in a fuller and clearly more official tone. "My lady, I ask, respectfully, that you consider the events since Nelson's change. If even one day, one hour, before he was beset any of those later occurrences were predicted to you, how would you have categorized those foretellings? Outrageous? Ludicrous? We are quite wholly in an environment in which the familiar will be no reliable reference. If you were not until now aware, you must be made so: The impossible is upon us."

"Mistress Blatatat," Lady Poon-Grebe said tentatively. "I have proclaimed my faith in your abilities and the unending support I am willing to devote to your task. But I must admit to an incomprehension at these preparations."

"Of course, your ladyship. I will explain: The forces at work at Castle Grundel are manifold and mighty. The spiritual realm is coextensive with our own. There are no gaps, blind spots, or unpopulated patches; but on the other hand, there are areas of greater activity. There are sites of great intensity, and Castle Grundel is most assuredly one. Castle Grundel is in fact a hive. The significance and history of this castle in our world is not one bit diminished in the others. And Nelson has fallen under the sway of such power."

"Are you not a countervailing power, Mistress?" Lady Poon-Grebe asked.

"I am a guide, ma'am, and over time have developed some, I will say, endurance. But for our purposes, no. I cannot contend alone with such a power here at work."

"But how are you aided by the addition of Lady Sauvignon? Or Lady Mantiss?" Vadney asked. "The one is a lusty nut entirely enthralled with any dirty mystic waving a forked stick — no offense, Mistress — and the other is on some crazed crusade to eliminate from life every delight familiar to man. The nobility's witchiest woman and the known-world's most indefatigable nag! How can they possibly help?"

"My lord, I am, I said, a guide. But I am also and perhaps more accurately a conduit. The unseen powers of the terrestrial and ethereal planes may travel through me. But like any portal or bridge I must draw strength from some support. I must be buttressed. That energy is all around and I have grown adept at bringing it into myself. But I must be forthright: The task I have before me is equal to that of the mythic Lucas of the Frosted Gauntlet."

" Oh, I love that tale! 'No man can eat 50 serpent eggs!' "

"Precisely, my lord. I use it as an illustration. The strength I need requires very specific sources. I am preparing, if you will, a recipe to fortify and sustain me, and as I do not yet know what I, what we, may face, I must be broadly prepared and provisioned."

"By this motley?"

"Yes. The Lady Sauvignon and her husband are known for their deep and ranging curiosities. I may draw upon that openness to venture more deeply into the remote; Lord and Lady Mantiss's opposed energy, their vigilant opprobrium, offers a well of resistance, of objection, which I may muster as defense, if necessary. Surely, Lord Poon-Grebe, you can recall any of the many victories of your vaunted ancestors. Would any have gone to battle with only lancers and no cavalry, or only cannons and no foot soldiers?"

"My ancestors would have gone to battle with nothing but flea bites and the chips on their shoulders," Vadney grumbled. "But I see your meaning."

"But what need have you of this journalist?" Lady Poon-Grebe asked.

Ekaterina stole a quick glance at Cyril, as if already in need of some cavalry.

"Again, I will be forthright and pray

your understanding. I could say that I will draw upon the spirit of the scribe for those very qualities you find so undignified, my lady: his ilk's cunning curiosity, their persistent prying, their oft-indecorous inquisitiveness. And those might be of some incidental benefit. But my immediate need is more practical and, I fear, egotistical. I wish to have the struggle documented."

Lady Poon-Grebe and, surprisingly, Ratch spoke as one: "In the newspapers?"

To Ekaterina's relief, Cyril piped in:

"If I may, your lord and ladyship, I think this is wise."

"Mr. Shakewit, how does the plight of my son, his private struggle, invite the attention of the masses?" Lady Poon-Grebe's question was the verbal equivalent of the white glove dragged across suspect mantle, inspected with a glittering eye and judged with a curled lip.

"My lady, you and Lord Poon-Grebe, as I have already said to him, are perhaps too modest to acknowledge the identification made between your family, families, and Maybia itself by the masses. Any assault on you is felt as an assault on us all."

Lady Poon-Grebe shifted in her seat, uncertain if she liked the flavor of this unfamiliar morsel.

"The brazenness of this, this event, the insult inflicted upon our, if I may, our first family — all respect to the King and Queen, of course — is of great national concern. Or would be, if known. What if this is just the advance guard of a ghostly force testing the preparedness of our, uh, inter-dimensional borders?"

Vadney and Camilla sent questioning looks toward Ekaterina, who responded with a gesture most easily translated as, "Hey, stuff happens."

Cyril continued, his voice becoming both martial and musical. "As your acclaimed ancestors have so staunchly, resolutely, unfailingly, unflinchingly defended and extended our great nation's vulnerable frontiers, our proud country's most tender bits, so, too, Lord Poon-Grebe should you be celebrated for your valor on this new and foreign front!"

His pitch shifted as he turned to address Lady Poon-Grebe. It became a soft, protective plea. "And your beloved Nelson — beloved by you first among many Maybians thankful for the continuation of such noble bloodlines — is a treasure whose welfare concerns us all. A treasure, the threat to whom will rouse in the hearts of our countrymen, once notified, such passion and concern and national fervor as to charge the air of Maybia with an energy to steel and armor Mistress Blatatat in the mightiest mail, arm her with the keenest, spiritual sword!"

The nobles were speechless and immobile. Ekaterina sat in mute anticipation. Cyril, too.

It was Ratch who finally broke the silence.

"I'd read that."

Cyril snapped his mouth open and quickly shut. Not quite quickly enough to prevent the escape of the single phrase.

"I know, right?!"

Castle Grundel bustled. Servants flitted throughout, purposeful and incurious. As lifelong (or longer: many came from families whose entire histories took place at the bottoms of grand staircases) professional domestics they were seasoned un-questioners, phlegmatic accepters of aristocratic caprice. Certainly among this population — for the staff was large — there were those of thoughtful mindsets, those to whom "why" was not wholly foreign, but class habits, daily exigencies and relentless overwork made infertile ground for such seeds of inquiry. Shoots were stunted far short of philosophical flower, producing mere rhetorical weeds: "What in the name of Cleon's Pleats . . . ?" then off to polish hooves or align all cutlery tines to the southwest.

    The personal proclivities of the lord and lady of this particular manor, too, had augmented the blasé preparedness for whim, be it in the name of indulgence or austerity. This was a staff ready for vision, revision and double vision. Still though, even manned by such a hardy and unaffected group, Castle Grundel had that day a charged and uncertain air.

Ratch, who presided over this efficient tumult as field marshall, was a notable exception to this inculcated cognitive dead ending. His own brain was every bit as busy as the castle's hallways, and Ratch found himself conflicted by the activity: The excitement was delightful, but worrisome. He berated himself for his anxiety. Had he not longed for some novelty, some interruption of his attendance upon Lord Poon-Grebe's cycles of dipsomania and dungeon upkeep? Well, here was that interruption in grand form, ushered in by these two characters he had himself retrieved from the lowest tavern in Boyledin: a flighty stand-up poet and a dubious mystic at whose words the whole castle hopped to! A flighty stand-up poet and dubious mystic who had the ears, it seemed, of both Lord and Lady Poon-Grebe.

Ratch barked out a correction to a young valet who might conceivably have been doing whatever it was he was doing incorrectly. It did not have the calming or empowering effect he had wished for.

The predictable behaviors of his lord and lady — yes, even Lord Poon-Grebe's idiosyncrasies had rhythms one could observe and learn — had given Ratch a sense of wisdom he now thought to be overstated. It stung his pride to feel his insight provincial, as it were, in the extreme.

He could not foretell the outcome of the activity unfolding around him, under the massive roofs he had come to think of as, in some way, his own. He was baffled in a place where he had for so long known certainty. He pondered as he briskly paced: What was at stake and for whom?

Reflexively, Ratch thought first of Lord Poon-Grebe. He had for so long been borne along those currents that he felt as tied to them as any sailor did to the waves and winds. True, too, that Lord Poon-Grebe's aims were by far the most scrutable: He wanted and had been promised the absence of his wife and stepson, and Lord Poon-Grebe was no meticulous planner. His thoughts likely went no further than the first weekend of that sweet deliverance. Though Ratch saw clearly enough that Cyril Shakewit had found some angle on his new-found familiarity with the nobleman, he could not fathom that angle and wondered if Cyril himself knew.

Lady Poon-Grebe was, as well, an easy read. She wanted, for perhaps the first time in their shared lives, the same thing as her husband: the reinvigoration and removal of her son, and herself, from Lord Poon-Grebe's presence. Ratch knew of her plans to enroll Nelson in the Sebastian Academy for Curious Boys (she was far more capable of thinking ahead than her husband) but also knew that physical separation was her ladyship's primary objective.

Mistress Blatatat was the main agent of these shared hopes. Mistress Ekaterina Blatatat, a woman with reputed powers of great formidability. Reputed. Ratch thought on Ekaterina's bearing, behavior and the information she had shared since her arrival at the castle. It was most suggestive of ability. But what ability, precisely? Had not he, himself, retrieved her from the Jakes &

Japes, of all places?

If she is a fraud, surely Cyril is an accomplice; and if they are frauds surely it will become evident and they will be exposed. And, now that this J. Mitchell Sludge has been invited, exposed as frauds to all of literate Maybia. But it was Ekaterina's own suggestion. Or is Cyril the brains behind it all?

Ratch found that last hard to believe.

Clearly no desired good (however obscure) could come but with the curing of Nelson. The known goals of Lord and Lady Poon-Grebe, and the risk of ruin for Cyril and Mistress Blatatat demanded this. What, then, would that mean for Ratch? How would his needs best be served? And for that matter, what were his needs? Ratch very much disliked this vertiginous feeling, this separation from his accustomed position as Lord Poon-Grebe's caretaker and confidant, his eyes, ears (and not infrequently inner ear). He wished for a happy resolution for Lord Poon-Grebe out of long-standing habit and understanding that his own ends were best served by bringing about his master's. But, unusually, Ratch was not in this case the means to those ends. In fact, he was uncertain what, exactly, the means might be. He experienced a fleeting temptation to call upon — whom? Cyril? Ekaterina? — someone to ask them directly, "What should I do?" But he could not overcome his wariness of those two and their evident but illegible agendas.

    Whatever was to happen, Ratch realized in that moment, he would have to shift for himself. Things were strange and getting stranger by the instant. He resolved to be opportunistic and alert.

He immediately thereafter seized the opportunity to administer constructive criticism to whichever domestic had left a carpet rolled across the threshold he had just attempted to cross. He critiqued expertly, he thought, from his back in a way that was still notably dignified, he was nearly certain.

Cyril's eyes stung.

"It smells like an apothecary arson in here."

"It will grow milder," Ekaterina said, distractedly.

"It will certainly capture the attention of the guests. Derangement of the sense, and all, right? Nice."

"Mmm. Not exactly, though it's helpful

to have them in sensitive states. But this isn't for them."

"Well, it can't be because you like it, can it?"

"It's a cleansing process, Cyril. I'm preparing the space for communication."

"How does that work?"

Ekaterina spoke like a gifted student still uncertain of her gifts and intimidated by her tutors. "The planes of existence are in many ways discrete. So much so that many disbelieve them altogether. Others find them credible but inaccessible, invisible. Some believe so readily that they misattribute every unexpected event to spiritual influence. A very few are — for who knows what reason —given glimpses enough to see that these planes, these myriad worlds, touch, jostle and overlap. Much as in our own world our learned investigators gain knowledge in fits and starts, never yet apprehending our dimension as a unity, ever yet puzzling its complexities, so these seers may have incomplete awareness yet know some things with great surety."

"Are you saying, 'It works because it works?'"

Ekaterina continued as if Cyril had not spoken, at all. "There are channels between the planes: people, places or objects who somehow reflect or echo into others. Some are more powerful than others. But there is much confusion among people: Every school child knows that the dockyards of the Sink are intensely mystical and haunted. Yet most, and adults, as well, mistakenly believe that graveyards are spectrally dense."

"They're not?"

"Well, of course not. If you're a restless

spirit what business would you have in a graveyard?"

"Fair point. Personally, I'd much rather be in a . . ."

"Tavern. Most haunted structures in Maybia."

"Well, I'll be. And the second?"

"Ancient castles once occupied by deeply troubled aristocratic families. There are some things that we who know — I'm discovering — just know. You know what's almost never eldritchly active? The area under a child's bed. Who'd go there? Silly. You know what is? Mirrors. You know what's almost never a sign? The weather. You know what almost always is? The behavior of cats."

"That actually makes a lot of sense."

"And this concoction of herbs produces an astringent smoke that should clear the space of all but the most purposeful presences and nettle them, so to speak, and stimulate the lingering latencies on this, their former plane, to speak, to make known their needs, their grievances, their demands or aims upon us."

Cyril took a moment to digest this, as Ekaterina caught her breath. When she had composed herself and again met his eye, he said:

"Really?"

Ekaterina pivoted her head, took in the entirety of the still-smoky chamber. She let her eyes linger on the prone and still-unresponsive mound that was Nelson Poon-Grebe.

"I'm pretty sure, yeah."

Ekaterina loomed like a Titan over a tiny landscape, yet felt closed-in upon and crowded. Illuminated by the flickering of numerous candles, the low ridges of the designs she had made with their drippings seemed to her like mountains in hard weather as viewed by the capricious creators of fickle climate, themselves. The tallow traces banked, mounted and meandered across the tectonic floor of the afflicted Poon-Grebe's enormous room. But the easy illusion of scale — indeed the very real sprawl of the chamber that assisted in the deceit of the eye — had no effect on Ekaterina. In all her years in Boyledin, from the greasy roil and churn of the streets of the Sink to the sweaty press of sour-breathed bonhomie at the Jakes & Japes, she had never felt so crowded, so bound by expectant presence.

"Stage fright," she rationalized, without conviction. It was more and different. "The insistent tug of a hoped-for future," she attempted a reasonable clarification, a more precise and personal but still prosaic explanation. It struck her as incomplete and sounded hollowly within her. The presence was nearer; it was, she thought, in a word the surprise of which gave way almost immediately to recognition and acceptance, "adjacent."

Nelson was in the room with her, of course. Pale to the point of luminosity, in the shimmering light he caught the eye like a subterranean pool (of the sort the stranded spelunker should well be wary, formed as they were with dramatic disproportionality between breadth and depth). The guests — Lord and Lady Mantiss, Lord and Lady Sauvignon, and the fuzzy little journalist J. Mitchell Sludge — had all arrived and been afforded the slow and traditional amenities of aristocratic hospitality. They would be escorted by Ratch into the bedchamber quite shortly. But these were not the arrivals heralded by Ekaterina's singing nerves. Her eyes blinked and it felt like shutters slamming chaotically in the storm gales of her breathing.

"Who do you want to be?" she thought loudly at herself, drowning out the gale and summoning (she could not help herself to think of it so) her inner Cyril: "Would Tessie Trewes be here, in the Castle Grundel? Ever? Never." Tessie Trewes was an energetic hustler, possessed of some little imagination and some great vague ambitions, but not the abilities to get her here. Tessie Trewes might — might — have managed to boost her Sink-bred survivor's instincts with Cyril's loopy philosophy of opportunism and make it to the victory at the Jakes & Japes with nothing else. But Tessie was too much of the Sink. Her story stopped there, surrounded by the delighted, dejected, disputatious, dipsomaniacal, downtrodden and dilettantish mess of regulars at Amateur Recitation Night. She began giving way earlier, as another made claims. That tavern victory was Tessie's crowning moment, and her ascent into the carriage of the Poon-Grebe's was her apotheosis. But it was not she who descended into the courtyard of the Castle Grundel, and it was not she who stood here nudged and prodded by energies the Sink residents regarded with only superstition or cynicism, each equally ignorant. It was not Tessie.

"Mistress Ekaterina Blatatat."

Ekaterina breathed deeply and evenly. She regarded Ratch without evident emotion as he admitted the full party for the night's activity. She met their eyes in turn, nodding a slight acknowledgment as the manservant guided them to the positions she had instructed.

First through the door was the journalist, Sludge, recognizable immediately by the great wooly wings of his mustache. On a larger man such follicular ornament might be suggestive of an heroic masculine solidity, but on Sludge's diminutive and fidgety frame it looked like smoky plumes from a small explosion just below or behind his nose, as if the same energy that kept him in a state of constant bodily pique had coursed through his cranium at velocity to blow his brains out his beak.

Lord Chutney Mantiss, the Earl of

Hertz-Nuptial, and his wife the Countess, Lady Prunella Mantiss, followed. If not for the differences in their garb one would be hard pressed to say which was which. It was not so much that they looked enough alike to be siblings but they looked enough alike to be bookends — bookends cast of disapproval and general intolerance. Their lanky frames were kept so rigidly upright they seemed ever so slightly to be leaning backward, entering the room as reluctantly as any biped vertebrate already in motion could possibly without coming to a full stop. Their heads reserved the right to judge and refuse entry until the last possible second. When their faces finally made it into the room one saw they were pinched as new shoes.

 The Vicomte and Viscountess de Louche —that is, the Puissian Lord Gaspar

Sauvignon and his Maybian wife Lady Mary Anne Sauvignon (nee Marionette) — sauntered a counterpoint entrance. Where the Mantisses were severe as the rules in a bookkeeper's ledger, the Sauvignons were the self-indulgent and profane marginalia in a schoolboy's text. They radiated an irreverent amused interest, an almost palpable hope that things might go just a bit off the track.

Cyril bustled through next, as ever seeming wholly out of place and completely untroubled by his displacement.

Finally, the Lord and Lady of the Castle Grundel arrived. In her time with them, Ekaterina had seen Vadney and Camilla to be no less eccentric, erratic and odd than any of the half-mad denizens of the scurrying, scheming streets of the Sink. But as Ratch closed the door behind them, sealing the company in the task at hand, Ekaterina's skin prickled as if she'd been suddenly cloaked in expressive eels. Vadney and Camilla were at that moment very much the Marquis and Marchioness of the d'Isle d'Eaux. Their foibles and frailties notwithstanding, the room was charged with the histories of their families, which were wellsprings and main currents of the history of Maybia. The Mantisses flared their nostrils, the Sauvignons widened their eyes, Sludge patted at his mustache as if trying to extinguish it, Cyril stared at their hosts in an attitude that might have been awed hunger (it was a "wow, that's a good-looking ham" kind of gaze), Ratch furrowed his brow and seemed to be performing desperate mathematics, like a merchant's apprentice with an off-brand abacus.

For his part, Nelson reclined and

respired with unwavering consistency.

"My lords and ladies, Mr. Sludge, Mr. Shakewit, Mr. Ratch, our endeavor today is dire. No less than a soul, and a much-loved . . ."

Vadney coughed slightly, then made a gesture toward the air with his fingers and eyes that conveyed something along the lines of "pesky throat elves, all over these days."

" . . . a much-loved soul, at that. It goes without saying that Lord and Lady Poon-Grebe are animated by the purest parental affection to return their son, Nelson, to his customary self . . ."

Ekaterina paused. Vadney froze, refusing to even blink.

"For that reason alone, I thank you on their behalf for your participation. Though you may have some lingering surprise or uncertainty about your inclusion, I can assure you that each of you contribute indispensably to the proceedings and greatly augment our chances of a happy outcome."

"Yes, as to that." J. Mitchell Sludge's voice, it turned out, was the very antithesis of his most noticeable physical characteristic. His mustache was billowy, atmospheric; his tone hard, clear, precise, virtually surgical. "The happy outcome. You say that the goal is to get the young Lord Poon-Grebe back to normal, as it were. And his current attitude is considerable relaxed — even by the common standards of youthful nobility."

Sludge's facial adornment twitched ingratiatingly at the edges as he turned his head to the assembled aristocrats. He resumed:

"But if I may say so, this is an unlikely

gathering in several specifics. Lord and Lady Sauvignon, you are known to go off the main track a bit, yeah? Your ladyship, in particular, has a reputation for an accommodating orientation toward the spooky stuff. Not to put too fine a point on it but it's said, respectfully, that your interaction with the otherworldly is more familiar than fearful. I had one fella tell me you cover the lunch breaks and vacation days of overworked spooks in castles from South Cliff to Tartan Notch."

"I am afraid you are misinformed," Lady Sauvignon responded. "I am fortunate to have as my fond acquaintances several souls of great spiritual sensitivity, but they are all quite corporeal." Lady Sauvignon's voice dropped at that last word, almost wistful. "While I have had some remarkable experiences of the, as you say, 'otherworldly' in their company, I have not, no, covered a, what was it, lunch break."

For his part the Vicomte de Louche merely gazed upon Sludge with an apparent amusement, as if watching a street performer's costumed monkey and awaiting his next tumble.

"No, course not, milady. My friend was likely speaking more colorfully than truthfully. You know how the rabble will babble. Plus it pleases a certain sort to speak knowing-like of our better families. That and the fact that you and the Vicomte have not been seen about much of late, till just recently. You spend much of your time in Puis, I understand."

At mention of his native city, the vicomte roused, "But of course! Puis is so much more entertaining! I swear, the weather in this country seeps into the very body. So gloomy."

"Puis is a most decadent city," bristled the Countess Hertz-Nuptial. "It is unserious in the extreme. Irresponsibility and frivolity reign. All evidence of an advanced state of decay."

"Oh, you have been?" the Vicomte beamed.

"Most assuredly, I have not!" the lady recoiled from the Puissian's smile. "There is nothing to be done for that corrupt city but to wait for its impending collapse. My husband and I dedicate our energies in our homeland, which though beset on all sides by pernicious influence, is made of stern stuff and may yet be defended from stain."

Sludge observed, "Your pursuit of civic and moral improvement on behalf of even the reluctantly improved is very well known, Lady and Lord Mantiss. More than a small surprise to find you here, in fact. I'd lay a wager that this surely is your first involvement in . . . well, what shall we call this? Is it a seance, an exorcism?"

All eyes turned to Ekaterina, and Lady Poon-Grebe loosed a cracked squeak of a sob. Lord Poon-Grebe looked at her in open curiosity, though for a moment only, then turned down the corners of his mouth in a nearly passable pantomime of step-parental worry.

"You may call it what you like, Mr. Sludge," said Ekaterina. "Though the terms you mention are hard and narrow."

"If I may, Mitch," Cyril interjected. He made brief eye contact with each of the attendees. "Mr. Sludge and I have a passing acquaintance, as we frequent some the same cultural institutions."

Lady Mantiss huffed.

"But if I may," Cyril continued, "Mistress Blatatat's abilities are of a nature that does not lend itself easily to categorization: seance, exorcism, eldritch conclave, paranormal parley . . ."

"Ooh, 'paranormal parley.' I like that," Sludge said, pulling a small notebook and pencil stub from his pocket. "Do you mind?"

"No, not at all. Bit of advice, though: Don't overdo the alliteration. Might seem affected. But where was I? Ah, yes! I have witnessed Mistress Blatatat employ her talents, her gifts, her — I am confident in terming them thusly — her powers on numerous occasions and can say truly they transcend the vernacular. To ask her to label them, fluent as she is in the tongue of terra incognito, is to ask the scholar to bark. Still, the populace deserves to know something of what transpires here and if anyone can reach them, it is you, Mitch. For you are as attuned to them as Mistress Blatatat is to this other more dimly known demographic. In your respective areas of expertise you are each, to put a word to it, conversant."

"So, this is to be a conversation, then? Homely term, that. Commonplace, even."

Lady Sauvignon spoke up, "Oh, but Mr. Sludge, there is nothing more common, if one only is aware. Creation is not so tawdry and limited as many would have you believe. The noisy preoccupations of the worldly, notwithstanding." She cast an unsubtle eye upon Lord and Lady Mantiss, at which Lady Mantiss uttered a sibilant syllable that would transcribed phonetically would be "fish" but inflected in such a way as to imply an especially hurtful type of fish.

"In my trade you learn fast to abandon

your ideas about what is and what ain't," Sludge said. "I've lost count of the things I've seen that would've shook a young Sludge right down to his too confident up-is-that-way core. So, let's say I'm not so dubious as Lord and Lady Mantiss. I'm still short of Lady Sauvignon's ease. Are you saying, Cyril, that the way to remedy whatever it is ailing young Nelson, there, is to simply rap on the dimensional door and shout, 'Oy, would you mind?! He's trying to have a childhood, here!'"

"Well, no, not 'simply,' Mitch. It's a not a simple conversation. But it is still a conversation., and those can take many a variable tenor. To take your own example: What are the possible outcomes when anyone raps on any door and begins a shouted conversation with 'Oy'? Quiet acquiescence might be the most-hoped for but it's hardly the most likely."

"I suppose that's true. 'Oy,' is usually followed by 'ow,' in my experience."

"Exactly so! Conversation. Give and take. Not demands, dialog. It's about building relationships." Here Cyril looked at Lord Poon-Grebe with what Vadney flounderingly assumed was intent. As the specific meaning did not quite make the full trip eye to eye, Vadney resorted to a tried-and-true gambit: "I hear you," he said.

"Gentlemen," Lady Poon-Grebe's voice dropped the temperature in the room two degrees. "Mistress Blatatat has assembled us all here for a very specific purpose. I must risk incivility because your private motives for participating interest me not one bit more than Mr. Sludge's inevitable, and inevitably horrid and vulgar, headline. I do not care if you have come out of compassion, curiosity or empty calendars. I do not care if this is described as a seance, a witchy ritual or a congress of crackpots."

"Ooh, those are fine turns of phrase, milady," enthused Sludge.

She continued without notice: "Mistress Blatatat, please, preparations have been painstaking and, it seems, quite thorough. I have put my faith in you and it has not wavered. But all the while Nelson's affliction endures and for all we know worsens. May we begin? May we please begin to help my son?"

"Yes, Lady Poon-Grebe. It is time. Please, be seated."

The party sat in the chairs provided, placed by Ratch at Ekaterina's direction. They were configured in the bedchamber's open space as an eight-pointed star, with Ekaterina standing at its center. Ratch stood at the closed door (in a tepid stew of awe and envy of finely dressed Cyril's place at the august seating arrangement), also as directed. Nelson breathed in a heap, habitually.

"If you will all look at the pattern of wax at your feet, you see a web of connection between us described. Each to each and all. I at its epicenter but not its aim. Allow your energy, whatever its tone — hopeful, hateful, skeptical, cynical — to follow those courses. Do not strive for influence. Do not concern yourself to obstruct. Simply feel as you feel, openly and unreservedly. Envision that energy flowing from you along those channels, swirling and mingling. Follow the paths with your eyes, see where they intersect, all tributaries feeding rivers, all flowing to the sea, to the undifferentiated depth, to the source beyond light, beyond reach, beyond ken."

"Wait, who's Ken?" Vadney asked, barely completing the question before a hiss like a paper cut from his wife silenced him. Ekaterina intoned on:

"Beyond comprehension. Follow the lines with your eyes and feel the currents they chart. Understand that these currents flow within larger currents, cosmic currents. Feel yourself borne along those currents."

The group did as told, their eyes performing tiny arabesques in their sockets. The ocular acrobatics and the still-astringent air combined with the lulling drone of Ekaterina's voice, producing in the guests various modes of relaxation evocative of personally favored bliss states:

Camilla felt her ears fill with the longed-for caterwaul, her arms with the yielding pudge, of her son again. The blood in

Vadney's veins warmed as if each swooping line of wax were a stream of exquisite vintage sipped leisurely in a dungeon of national notoriety. The Viscountess de Louche felt herself awash in social attention, clamored for, and swept along an endless open invitation. Her husband, of sensual pleasures envisioned by many, afforded by few and admitted by almost none. Lady Mantiss was transported by a surge of gratitude. Not her own for an object or outcome but by that of others for her: the adoring indebtedness of childlike masses thankful for her salubrious supervision and moral custodianship. Lord Mantiss, too, was enraptured by a scenario of appreciation. Specifically, of his wife saying just two words, even once: "Not bad." J. Mitchell Sludge felt the value of his own written opinion elevated to that of the Kingdom's greatest resource, prized over every powdered wig in parliament and all the cannons and canvas in the Royal Navy. Cyril's head echoed with an enduring ovation the like of which no auteur, adventurer nor executioner had yet received. And Ekaterina felt this all.

She felt this at first as a trickle, insights and sensations as particular and fleeting drops. But it grew steadier, beading, streaming till she was coursing in full flood. She struggled against the urge to dam; she broadened her banks. She became a reservoir, and still received. She overran. She broadened further. She became the sea. She became the undifferentiated depth. And from that depth, from beyond the light, from beyond reach, from beyond comprehension, there came a voice:

"Oy, now, what's all this, then?"

G.E.N.I.U.S. & Magic

Most of the individuals seated around Ekaterina had known her only a short time and, none, save Cyril for more than just a few days. Every one of them was quite certain, however, that the voice that had uttered that question could not possibly have been Ekaterina's own. This was in itself troubling, for it was very clearly Ekaterina's own mouth, still located quite evidently on Ekaterina's own face, on the very same head she'd been using these past days. These curiosities notwithstanding the on-lookers, or on-hearers, could not help but note that the voice was rather more cheerful, even playful, than their short acquaintance would lead them to expect of her, and considerably more suggestive of a quite largish man. Likely bearded.

"Isn't this quite a to do?" the good-natured, ill-housed (for surely such a full and sonorous noise must be cramped in so modest a frame!) barreled on. "The very quality is here, ain't it?"

It was Ekaterina, herself, who first regained composure, which fact only advanced the state of her companions' dis- , as she spoke in her native, familiar tone to converse with that other.

"Welcome," she said. "To whom are we so fortunate as to address ourselves?"

"Well, well. Aren't we formal and polite? 'Whom,' indeed!" A basso chuckle burbled from Ekaterina's lips. "I was known by some — for a time, that is — as William Wagstaff. More familiarly as Big Billy, and often enough as Big Belly. So, we needn't stand on ceremony as I was never much used to it and certainly have no need of it, now."

"Billy, then. Do you speak to us from beyond?"

"Beyond? Do you mean, am I dead?"

"Well . . . if it's not rude to ask, yes."

"As a mackerel, my dear. No need to be delicate. I'm not sensitive about it. But, true enough, it don't suit everyone."

"Billy, can you tell us what you seek here?"

"Seek? Well, nothing really. I just heard the racket you were making — swirling energy and suchlike — and thought I'd pop in. The things you corpses get up to, usually good for a laugh."

Cyril was the first of the others to find his own voice. "Uh, we corpses, Billy?"

"Oh, yeah. That's what we call you pre-deads. Short for 'corporeal.' Funny, yeah?"

The slowly rousing group muttered a semi-articulate affirmative noise. Vadney even managed, "Good one." Sludge scribbled in his notebook.

"So, now, what's the occasion? What has you poking around this side of things? Party game? Reaching out to a departed pet? Looking for tips on betting this year's Stumbletown Steeplechase?"

"No, Mr. Wagstaff," Lady Poon-Grebe spoke. "It's something quite serious."

"Serious as the grave, eh?" Billy spoke with what was surely a self-satisfied smile. "Good thing you've got this one, then." Ekaterina's hands gestured to herself. "Not many of you corpses make it as easy as her. Not that I mind slamming doors, mucking about in mirrors or speaking through cats, mind you. It's all great fun. But this is a pleasant break from routine, I'll own. So, what is it, this serious business you're about?"

"My son, Mr. Wagstaff. My son, Nelson, is grievously affected by spiritual influence and has become insensate, numb to this world and unreachable even to his own devoted, distraught mother's love. Can you release him, Mr. Wagstaff? Free him, as you seem still possessed of the light of human compassion."

"Oh, dear," responded Billy, not unkindly. "I'm afraid I can't help you on that one. Not that we on this side never do you pre- types a good turn. It's not all bump-in-the-night stuff, you know. That would get dull right quick. But I really just stopped in for a moment, just now. I've had nothing to do with your son. He's not mine to free, y'see."

Ekaterina's voice returned to ask, "To

whom can we appeal, Billy? If you cannot act on our behalf, can you offer guidance?"

"Hmm. Well, I don't know. We don't usually grant favors quite so directly. Some of the B'zerki sprites go in for that sort of thing: loafing about in bottles, and such, waiting to grant highly conditionally wishes. All seems a bit nit-picky to me. Who wants to die then go into contract law, I ask! We tend a bit more toward signs and portents, if you know what I mean: visitations that may be dreams, half-remembered riddles in verse, furniture and furnishings disarranged meaningfully. It's a more poetic approach, I feel. Still, feels a waste to make an appearance and leave you with nothing. What'd you say your son's name was?"

"It's Nelson. Nelson Poon-Grebe."

"Nelson Poon . . . Not that lot!"

Vadney started. "What was that?"

Big Billy's voice had lost much of its fullness. "My, my. Look at the time. How it flies. Yes, yes. Even here beyond time, and all. Late for one's own afterlife, as they say. I really should toddle off."

Camilla cried out pitifully.

Vadney stammered, "Well, now, here, hold on . . ."

The Vicomte de Louche made a recognizably Puissian noise of bored disappointment and superiority. His wife pouted.

The Mantisses sniffed in unison.

All to no effect.

But Cyril said, "That's hardly poetic."

"Well, now, look here," Big Billy protested. "It's just that . . ."

"Signs and portents. Ha!" Even Lord Sauvignon took admiring note of Cyril's condescension. "Nothing very enigmatic about running away. 'I really should toddle off?' Makes B'zerki fine print seem like the verse cycles of Lopar the Loquacious."

"Now, that's just hurtful!" Big Billy's voice cracked with inter-dimensional insult. "All right, fine, then. I'll see if I can come up with something. But these are not ideal conditions. You're really putting me on the spot. And I'm not sure why you're going to such efforts, anyway. You know, you're not-alive quite a bit longer than you are alive. Even if you get Nathan . . ."

"Nelson," several corrected.

" . . . Nelson back, it's just for a minute, relatively speaking. And speaking of relatives . . . . Well, forget it. It's your seance. All righty. I've got something. OK, here we go:

Whomsoever has forbearance

  of standard, grand- , and great-grandparents
   has never met the likes of these
   who ring 'round young Nelson Poon-Grebe.
   But hope yet ye for a happy progeny
   To thrive beneath an assumèd heraldry:
   A step was made, the step must take
   and step taken, step-maker, he must vacate!"

  Big Billy's voice rose and swelled as he orated, very nearly resuming his earlier warmth and vigor. He concluded, paused and cleared his throat. Or, Ekaterina's throat, confoundingly.
  "Wasn't bad, given the circumstances, I think," he said quietly filling a silence he seemed somehow to resent.
  "It was okay," Cyril said.

"Okay? Unprepared and under pressure? I was just visiting! Be fair!"

"It was okay, I said! Not bad. That 'these-Grebe' rhyme was a bit strained . . ."

"Oh, and who do we have here? Maybia's Poet Laureate? Hark, everyone! Gather 'round! We have here, no doubt, the finest versifier in the land! It's the Venerable Boob!"

"Listen, you! I never said I was a tremendous talent, but I'm no slouch, either!"

"You don't give yourself enough credit. I'm sure you're a tremendous . . ."

"Are you kidding? Just how long have you been dead? That joke was old when Maybia was just a forest full of men taking turns hitting each other with hammers! No offense to your family, Lord Poon-Grebe."

"Oh, none taken, Cyril. The Poon-

Grebes of old were certainly a temperamental batch."

"And, as it happens, as I was saying, I've scribbled a rhyme in my time."

"Oh, have you now? Couplets as ambitious as 'rhyme' and 'time'? How daring."

"That was just a coincidence! Rhymes like 'wine-dark sea' and 'buggery,' and in terza rima, at that!"

"Really? I don't believe you."

Cyril turned to Ratch and then Sludge, both of whom offered gestural support, which Billy apprehended through the borrowed network of Ekaterina's nervous system, one supposed.

"Well, that's pretty good, really." He sounded sad. "But then you don't know what I know. I shouldn't even be sticking around here. A Poon-Grebe, of all things.

Was just out for a laugh. I should keep more to myself. Communicating with you corpses directly is always so chancey. For every one delightfully lissome lass with a morbid streak there're a half-dozen hectoring clerics, three nervous spinsters reeking of garlic, two boon seekers and now a precocious needling poet! Well, I've learned my lesson. Good luck with your adventures in the afterlife, corpses. You'll need plenty."

Big Billy's voice grew both softer and hollower, like he were walking down a long, echoey hallway. Before he faded out altogether, he was stopped by a sharply shouted, "Hey!"

"What? Who's that?" Billy asked faintly.

"It's Sludge. When you said that thing about the Stumbletown Steeplechase . . ."

Big Billy's answer, if he made one, was inaudible. But the air in the room gained a sudden static charge that shocked Sludge when he tugged his mustache. And when Ratch opened the door at the sound of a soft scratching, a tabby cat for whom all present denied ownership or familiarity padded in and relieved itself calmly on the journalist's left foot before padding right back out.

In reaction, Sludge merely sighed and tore a page out of his notebook, which he used to wipe his boot tip.

"It was worth a shot."

The conscious inhabitants of the room began talking all at once: a welter of words as intricate as the wax circuits mapping their energetic involvement. Excitement, bafflement, speculation, interpretation all bubbled, giving way one to the other. In the noise and confusion, no one noticed Ekaterina sag toward the slate.

Moments later, she was limply fending

off the attentions of the assembly from Cyril's chair, where he had placed her after retrieving her from the floor with fraternal care.

"I am fine. I am fine. You must take my word for it."

"You collapsed like empty clothes."

"Cyril, I am perfectly well, thank you. When William departed it was just a bit like letting the air out of a balloon. I was unprepared, that is all."

Lord Sauvignon asked, "We should allow you to rest after such an exhibition, no? Shall we have you brought to your room?"

"No, there is no need. Just a glass of water, perhaps."

"Ratch," Lord Poon-Grebe shouted after the departing servant, "something, too, from the cellars! Something bracing. For

Mistress Blatatat, of course."

Lady Poon-Grebe countered firmly, "Bring whatever Mistress Blatatat requests to her room, Ratch." Then more gently to Ekaterina, "Mistress, you must rest. The strain on you is evident."

"But Nelson . . ."

"Yes. Nelson. I must not squander or abuse the hope that the spirit says still exists. I may not allow you to push beyond your limit. Without you, Nelson is lost. Without you, I am lost. Please, retire and restore your strength. We will resume when you feel yourself to be fully ready."

"No rush, I think," said the vicomte. "Were he propped upright, clad for sport and chased by upperclassmen, I'd still wager that boy's no sprinter."

"I'd wager, on the other hand, quite a bit on Lady Poon-Grebe — in almost any contest or combat. Had she been so fortunate as to have been born or married into a Puissian family she'd have been a legend in the ring. She has a most ferocious aspect."

Vicomte de Louche's tone was appreciative and sincere, tones not common to Puissians, individually. Coupled thusly it was quite a rare event. The males of the party had retired to a sitting room to drink and talk while waiting out Ekaterina's recovery.

"The 'ring,' Lord Sauvignon?"

"Yes, you know, the fighting ring."

Sludge offered, "I reckon Lord Sauvignon is referring to the Festival of Feminine Fisticuffs and Grand Opera Ball, Cyril. Annual debutante thing."

"They fight?"

"Of course! Like wet cats. Our noble women are not made of china, to be introduced to society wrapped in tissue, as if purchased from a department store."

"Puis is a most singular city, my lord."

"Thankfully so," said Lord Mantiss.

"Oh, now, Mantiss" began Vadney.

"No, no, Poon-Grebe. Though I am not surprised to suspect that you excuse or even condone the moral depravity of that indolent, luxurious city. But I must hope — and strive toward this end — that it remains singular, at least."

"Luxurious, it is," said Sludge. "Dunno about indolent, though. I used to be Foreign Society Correspondent. Been to a couple of those balls, and agree that Lady Poon-Grebe would make a good showing. Not sure that I'd put money on anybody else in this castle, though. Self included."

"It's outrageous! Noble women brawling like tavern wenches in finery, and then attending the opera, proudly and luridly bruised and bloodied!"

"It's rough, I'll give you that." Sludge responded. "But the state of the audience — half battered and, all, shall we say, excitable, and none able to sit still comfortably — does contribute to markedly shorter operas than is the norm."

The men, even Mantiss, murmured acknowledgement at that inarguable good.

"A sight shorter, speaking of, than this 'conversation,' as you termed it, Cyril, is likely to be," he continued. "And I'm still unclear, as I think my readers would be, on the make-up of this spooky little salon. Mistress Blatatat's explanation, energies and such, is a bit arcane for a simple city scribbler such as myself. I can't help but think there are other more down-to-earth motivations. Not to press, Lord Mantiss, but what are you doing among the ghosts and, weirder still, no insult intended to our gracious hosts, among the Poon-Grebes?"

Vadney smiled blithely at the mention of his name, for he had not really been listening.

One might typify the Earl of Hertz-Nuptial's response as "podium implied."

"My wife aside, Mr. Sludge, my one supreme love is Maybia, the greatest nation that has ever been. And what is a nation without borders? What is a culture without rules? What is a race without tradition? Lady Mantiss and I are devoted to the preservation of all that makes Maybia great. That commitment requires sacrifice at times; a willingness to be at the front lines, as Mr.

Shakewit suggested these might be. Wherever those grand and necessary traditions, rules and borders are threatened."

"As they were when the vicomte, here, was admitted to the Misplaced Rake?"

"Quite so. A Puissian in Maybia's oldest club? It's preposterous. What next, B'zerkis?"

"Yes. I remember your wife saying much the same thing outside the club. And, yet, you were attempting to gain entry for Lady Mantiss, were you not? And, Lord Poon-Grebe, the club is quite solid in its prohibition of women, correct?"

"I should say so!"

"So, Lord Mantiss, why the fuss over the admission of Lord Sauvignon?"

"Well, I've already said! He's Puissian! My wife is a lady, of course, but she is a

Maybian lady! To admit a foreigner before a Maybian?! Outrageous."

"You use that word quite a bit. Clearly, you are outraged. And I think perhaps I'm catching on. You've been told, as have we all, that Mistress Blatatat has formed this group in this peculiar shape to improve her chance at pushing back whatever or whomever back across the barrier they've crossed into Nelson. And these, let's call them 'spirits,' they're . . ."

"Well, Mr. Sludge, presuming that this whole rigamarole isn't some perverse pantomime and that these, yes, spirits exist, they're certainly not our kind, are they?"

"I s'pose not, my lord. I s'pose not. And you, Lord Sauvignon? One presumes you're rather less rigid in the notion of borders, etcetera? Yet, you earlier expressed a partisan fondness for your native land. Why join the most venerable, even representative, club of such a cold, dour country?"

"For the same reason we are in attendance, now: Mostly just to please my Maybian wife. As a friendly aside, my dear Mantiss, you might consider taking your own wife on a trip to my city. I find that Maybian women transplanted there flower most surprisingly and delightfully. In fact, the viscountess has earned herself a sterling reputation at the festival. The first lady of Maybian heritage ever to do so! Many a young noblewoman has prayed to draw another and avoid the quick left hand of my love. Results vary, of course, and you might not be so lucky. But what have you got to lose?"

That Lord Mantiss thought little of that plan was as clear as Lord Sauvignon's delight that he did.

"But, Mr. Sludge, you are mistaken about my regard for prescriptions: I adore them, prohibitions of all types. For there is nothing so amusing as the panic and confusion of their devotees when they are broken or used against them. So, I, for one, hope this visitation is extended and credible enough to continue to trouble my new friends the Earl and Countess of Hertz-Nuptial. Of my many, this may be my chiefest pleasure: to see the conservative of middling intellect and inflexible imagination tortured."

Vadney perked up: "Did someone say 'torture?'"

"I think you're bearing up awfully well, Camilla. But it must be a terrible strain. I pray that Mistress Blatatat's evident power gives you hope."

Ekaterina nodded slightly in receipt of the compliment. The ladies were seated in a room just off the bedchamber that had been given her by the Poon-Grebes. She had insisted that she did not need sleep, and would be restored by a few moments in a comfortable chair with tea.

"Though I am heavy yet with the deprivation of my son, I am indeed heartened, Mary Anne. And I must thank you, particularly. Without you, I might never have known of Mistress Blatatat's astonishing gifts. And, Pru, thank you, too. I understand — too well — that your sensitivity to the moral health of the nation smarts at the mere contemplation of my and Mary Anne's husbands' . . ."

"Now, Camilla, I must say that my Sauvignon has some points about . . ."

"I mean no offense, Mary Anne. Today of all days, I do not find fault. I only wish to express gratitude that for whatever reason, despite whatever possible objection, you have both come."

"Oh, Camilla, how could we have done otherwise? We are here to help, course. But, also, this is such a momentous event," Lady Sauvignon's voice swelled with emotion. "To witness she who will surely become the foremost mystic of our era in direct contact with manifest travelers from the realms beyond!"

"And to let them know with stern clarity that they may turn right back around, thank you very much," Lady Mantiss's voice swelled too, but more in the manner of military brass. She added in a muted coda, "And, yes, of course, to help."

Ekaterina spoke. "My ladies, if I may,

please. Your opinions are your own, of course, and must needs proceed from your convictions. Lady Sauvignon may most eagerly anticipate a kind of exchange arrangement with the otherworldly. Lady Mantiss, you may most fervently wish for parties on all sides of these shifting frontiers to become the staunchest of homebodies. Neither wish is wrong; neither is relevant. There is no 'should,' here, and we do not have standing to dictate terms. Our aim is reclaim a contested site: Nelson. As yet, we do not know why he has been claimed, nor by whom. If we are both effective and lucky, we may be granted audience."

She addressed Lady Mantiss: "It is not a protest rally."

And then Lady Sauvignon: "It is not a key party."

"What, pray, is a key party?" asked Lady

Mantiss.

"Oh, it's when guests at a weekend gathering in a country house take all the bedchamber keys . . ."

"Countess de Louche." Ekaterina said, softly but purposely.

"No, of course. Another time, Pru."

Lady Poon-Grebe ignored the digression: "But, Mistress, I don't understand. An audience? Are we to petition these whatever they are? These interlopers? To bargain? What could they want from us? From Nelson?"

"I don't know, my lady. But that is what I must discover and what I must attempt to negotiate."

"Negotiate? Negotiate with what? If these are truly the dead to whom we speak, what could they want of us, what could we offer? William said it was only your unusual power that made conversation so easy — I do not slight the effort you have exerted, Mistress."

"Thank you, Lady Poon-Grebe. But I am recovering quickly, and I believe I grow stronger with experience."

"I am happy to think so. But with even your abilities, increasing as they may be, can we treat with these entities as equals? The desires that motivate us on this side of death must mean little to them: wealth, land, possessions. Surely, not these."

"I am hesitant to guess, my lady. But I believe we may suspect from William's riddle, if that's what it was, that some action in this realm is desired."

"Camilla, if I may offer a perspective, something I have learned from from dear husband and from my time in Puis. We in Maybia do so value those things you've mentioned: physical fortunes of one sort or another. We go to great and violent lengths to obtain them and great and showy lengths to display them. The Puissian temperament is somewhat different. It is — I say this as a Maybian, still — subtler. Oh, they like their things well enough, as we all know. But what they love most, I have come to realize, is influence, the ability to alter the course of things. My dear Gaspar absolutely delights when he feels he has nudged things out of their customary or predictable progress."

"The Puissian style and direction of influence rankles me to the very core, and causes me great concern for you personally, Mary Anne," Lady Mantiss snipped. "But I think you may have seized upon something. Influence — by no means a skill foreign to Maybians — is a powerful drive. It is precisely this that Chutney and I have dedicated our own lives to achieving. We aim to influence Maybians to protect our home, our culture, our national soul from — I am sorry, Mary Anne —the rival influences of the likes of your husband and his countrymen, among others. Perhaps, the spirits seek similarly to affect some change upon Maybia through the Poon-Grebes, through Nelson. We must be vigilant! We must not compromise our character! Maybia for Maybians!"

Lady Poon-Grebe turned from her friends imploring eyes. "Mistress Blatatat?"

"Whether the motives are prankish or political I cannot say, my lady. And for our purposes at the moment it is pointless to speculate. All we can do is ask and hope we are up to whatever is asked of us in return."

At which all three noblewomen shivered very differently expressive shivers.

When the party was again convened in Nelson's room, anticipation mounted to a level more common to much larger gatherings: sporting events or popular protests just, just, just this side of riot. "Ooh, you know what would make this moment absolutely perfect?" the air asks. "A carelessly lobbed brick!" it answers itself.

Their positions resumed, the participants stared attentively at Ekaterina, standing again at the hub of the wax design. The circumstances lent themselves to attentiveness, of course, and for some of the attendees it was the default state. Viscountess de Louche invited experience with almost amatory eyes; the Marchioness of d'Isle d'Eaux's habitual raptor's glare glittered; the Countess of Hertz-Nuptial's evangelical gaze was straight and humorless as a rank of Crusaders. But even those whose typical temperaments were less focused were at this moment rapt: Sludge's mustache for once seemed less than a skeptical hedge and more like alert antennae; the Vicomte de Louche lacked all languidness; Lord Poon-Grebe very nearly resembled a St. Juicy's pet pupil; and Cyril did not appear to be hosting a three-ring circus, a dog fight and an extended-family St. Grog's Day drinking challenge in his head simultaneously.

At the door, Ratch was occupationally attentive, but even more so. Nelson, alone, was peaceful. Peaceful as the dew-sequined dawn meadow before the bugle is blown and the cavalry and cannon churn it to muddy, gutty ruts. He looked quite sweet.

At Ekaterina's prompt, they followed the wax patterns with their eyes. Once again, they looped and scrolled as she intoned. They slipped more quickly than before, even eagerly, into their transports, dropping defenses and opening themselves for visions of desires fulfilled. Ekaterina felt herself awash, enlarged, oceanic. One would be tempted to say that her head filled with a roar, for that's a phrase easily consumed, but it was not so. Her head could not be said to contain anything, any more than existence can be said to be filled with southwest. Her head, her being, became the roar. It was the exact opposite of a near-death experience. Ekaterina was briefly obliterated by a near-everything experience. But she got better. (Or worse, depending upon your personal perspective on the appropriate integrity of individual being-ness versus transcendent pan-dimensional unity. Different strokes.)

With effort, she reassembled a distinct consciousness enough to listen and to attempt to appreciate distinct detail. No sociable spirit, no ambassadorial Big Billy stepped forward.

But the roar began to reveal intricacies, contours if not patterns. Over the (were they moments that passed? Millenia?) elapsed time, Ekaterina tasted shapes, smelled alien equations, felt incomprehensible music brush her skin (was that her skin?). Her heart, let's call it, beat like a star, her blood surged like the birth of a new species, her lungs filled with the dust of a dynasty's collapse. Finally:

"Just because we're dead doesn't mean we have time to kill. Are you just about done with your sightseeing?"

There is a feeling one has when after

traveling in foreign lands one encounters a countryman and thrills at the tones of one's native tongue and finds one's home accent sweeter than the most exotic delicacy. This was not like that.

Instead, Ekaterina found the gruff and indisputably Maybian voice jarring and uncomfortable in the extreme.

"My sightseeing? No. Well, that is, yes. But I wasn't . . . I can be . . . if . . . who is this?"

Multiple voices, all Maybian, spoke at once and over each other.

"I told you this jiggery-pokery was a waste."

"Should we have spent our time rattling chains, you old fool?"

"'A powerful seer,' you said. 'Let's have an air of mystery,' you said."

"You've been dead barely a century!

What do you know?"

"If it had been left to you, we'd be cavorting about like bloody school boys trying to spook each other after lights out. Throw a sheet over yourself, why don't you?"

"Could we not have just written a note?"

"What are we, secretaries?!"

"Enough."

The last voice boomed with the weight of ages and the others went still.

"Show her."

In something shorter than an instant the perplexing complexity snapped into sharp focus and Ekaterina found herself in a very specific place and in quite specific company. If anything, it was more confusing than before.

She stood in Nelson Poon-Grebe's bedchamber still surrounded by those whom she had gathered for the seance. The room was in every detail as it had been when last visible to her, save the utter and remarkable immobility of those companions and the distinct and unsettling vitality of twelve new chamber mates gathered around the bed of the youngest Poon-Grebe.

"Is it the legs?" one of the imposing figures asked.

Ekaterina stammered, "I'm sorry?"

"The legs. I expect we're familiar to you passingly, but from the legs up."

She blinked and refocused. Standing before her were the dozen previous, historical/legendary Marquises d'Isle d'Eaux. She swept her eyes across them and a cognitive echo of a gallery wall pinged in her otherwise vacant-feeling head. She performed the sweep a second time, in reverse and lower.

"Yes. The legs," she said, without really knowing why she was saying anything, at all.

The men before her were of varying statures and degrees of beardedness. Their costumes reflected the progression of Maybian eras from mere violent island to vast modern empire. But there was a perceptible thread, a kind of uniformity to the men. Ekaterina wondered if it were more the Marquisity or the Poon-Grebishness that made them categorical, despite the more-than-just-years difference between the massive, glowering brutal-beard-bearing monster at one end of the row and the more modestly proportioned and suavely clean-shaven man at the other. It was the latter who spoke now.

"We are, as I'm sure you realize, the Marquises d'Isle d'Eaux, and we welcome you and thank you for your attendance."

A gruff rumbling — a mutter that sounded like a storm — came from the most massive marquis, but the speaker continued in his own soft and stately voice.

"It has been agreed that I should serve as spokesperson for our purposes here, by reason of temporal proximity. It is, judging from your appearance, likely that you and I shared some brief overlap in our respective embodied existences. I should like to introduce myself, formally. I am, or was, Lord Hilary Clare Bristol Poon-Grebe, 12th Marquis d'Isle d'Eaux and, though it discomfits me to say so, father of the current, your acquaintance, Vadney."

"Thank you, my lord. My lords. I am honored to be in your company and hope to be of use to you and to the current lord of Castle Grundel, who is . . ."

"As useful as a scabbard full of spoon!" roared the left-most marquis.

"Please," resumed the right-most, calmly. "As I said, it has been agreed that I shall conduct this parley, as it were."

The vocal noble quieted but the ether around him burned blue.

"Mistress Blatatat, we have — well, not 'brought,' that would be too strong — but influenced you here in hopes that you are the one to assist us in a most important effort. I am pleased beyond expression at your capabilities thus far, and more confident than ever that your reputation is merited."

Ekaterina clung to deference like flotsam in a sea of total bafflement. "Yes, my lords. I surmise, then, that you have exerted some spiritual suggestion upon Lady Poon-Grebe, who delivered your summons."

"That harridan's fit for delivering nothing but harangues to weak-willed husbands!"

Ekaterina was spared the effort of delicate response by the soothing tones of the most freshly dead marquis.

"Ah, yes. Camilla's desire to have you at Castle Grundel was an element of our, call them, arrangements. And it may be that her ends may by satisfied by our own; but they are not identical, and you've not yet heard ours."

Clinging grimly to this barely buoyant politesse, the horizons seemed ever-more distant. There was no landfall in sight. "But I would assume, is your aim not to restore Lord Nelson to himself?"

"My word, no! What a terrible proposal. Restore? As he was? Mistress Blatatat, it was we elder Poon-Grebes who put him in this state."

"Should we poke her, or something?"

The rest of the group looked at Vadney and did not, he noticed (pleased), immediately deride his idea. They then looked back to Ekaterina, at whom, prior to Vadney's delightfully unmolested query (very pleased, really), they had been staring for something like fifteen minutes.

Ekaterina stood at the center of her wax arena. She looked relaxed and poised. But in that quarter hour she had not spoken a word nor moved, save the slow blink of her eyes and the gentle bellows of her breath.

"Might be a good idea. She looks concussed," said Sludge. "Saw a fella like that in the Jakes & Japes one night. Fancy sort, a real dude. See, he tried to compliment Dolly on her 'assiduity,' the poor showoff. At any rate, it's dangerous to let 'em doze, I'm told."

"She looks quite all right to me," said Lady Sauvignon. "Like she's in a lovely bubble bath."

"Her look of transport calls to mind less the scented herbs of the bath and more the so-called sacred herbs of the East."

Lady Poon-Grebe responded tartly, "Vicomte de Louche, this is no inebriate's indulgence. Mistress Blatatat is engaged in something consequential."

"I beg your pardon, Lady Poon-Grebe. You mistake me. Certainly, we all know, by reputation, of course, the smoke-filled dockside dens where sailors, ruffians and others explore exotic temptations or compulsions. But I thought first of the B'zerki Caliph's Floral Warriors. It is said that they, in an induced state, too, serve as guides between the living and the dead. Though it was exclusively introducing the former to the latter. Quite a consequence, I would say."

"She looks more like a sleepwalker to me," said Lord Mantiss. "Why aren't there voices, like before? Maybe she's just dozed off?"

"Oh, well, you can't wake a sleepwalker, everyone knows that," said Vadney. "It can sort of break them, or something. Ratch, what was it you were telling me? Who was it, Lady Fiddlehead's nephew? Who was woken from a dream and thereafter would lap milk from a bowl and answer only to 'Boots'?"

"I would not like to speak indiscreetly, sir, but there was a family of some note in the West Counties whose household expenditures for cat grass were remarked upon frequently, if in hushed tones, after an event quite similar to that you have described."

J. Mitchell Sludge scribbled maniacally. "Hey, that's great stuff!"

Cyril opined, "Well, I think it would be a very bad idea to interrupt Mistress Blatatat. She knows what she is doing and, more to the point, we really, really don't."

The group could not debate the point.

"What, then, do we do in the meantime?" Lady Mantiss asked.

"Hey, Ratch," called Sludge. "Anyone else of note spoken of in frequent tones, if hushed?"

"But why?" Ekaterina asked, her mind suddenly less a sober counselor and more a comedy duo short one straight man.

"Well, as an invitation, of course," said Lord Hilary Poon-Grebe.

"To whom?" The now-desperate solo act in Ekaterina's head devolved into a pointless series of pratfalls.

"To you, Mistress. We wanted to speak to you. We have something quite important to arrange and we are hopeful of your participation."

"Is this dainty blather to be never-ending?" The civil exchange was trampled under the near-stampede of a shout from the mountainous marquis. "Parley and palaver! Is this a tea party? Are we hostesses? Tell the witch what we want — or must you yet ask her to dance?"

"Mistress Blatatat, may I introduce my

most esteemed great-great-great-great-great-great-great-great grandfather, Lord Leslie Evelyn Aubrey Poon-Grebe, the first Marquis d'Isle d'Eaux."

"You listed all those 'greats' just to annoy me, you chatty twerp," grumbled Leslie.

"I did, sir," his descendent replied with a smile. "But I admit, Mistress, that my forebear has a point. There are times when niceties are best abbreviated. I shall be succinct."

"Ha!" a single thunderclap boomed in the left of the room. But the spokesmarquis paid no mind.

"Mistress Blatatat, I pray it does not strike you as immodest to suggest that we, the now-historical Marquises d'Isle d'Eaux have had some role in the establishment of our home country."

"Most certainly not, my lord! Your

lordships are as much Maybian history as . . ."

"As windy politicians shaved close as courtesans?" rumbled Leslie Poon-Grebe.

"Yes. And as mud-caked thugs trading in violence and lice," answered an unflappable Hilary. "We were, in our times, and in our ways, we think, effective agents of what has become a quite grand empire."

"None could deny it, my lord."

"You will not be surprised, then, to hear that the continued success of the nation remains important to us even in death. We have strived that it should long outlive us and that the Poon-Grebe name should long be linked with that of Maybia's grandeur."

"Certainly, it will, my lords! How could it be otherwise?"

Ten of the twelve marquises shifted uncomfortably, their attentions directed suddenly away from their agreed-upon representative — while one stared a pummeling of a stare at the same. For his part, Lord Hilary Poon-Grebe sighed, then answered.

"In a word: Vadney."

"No!" Vadney exclaimed. "It can't be."

"My sources are close to the family and quite usually reliable, sir," said Ratch.

"Are you expecting us to believe that Lord Drat's, the Earl of Slipshodshire's, Order of Maybian Greatness, his OMG, was awarded to procure his silence?" Lord Mantiss's voice rose in pitch until it was almost insectile.

"Not precisely, sir. I am saying only that a noblewoman from a notoriously disordered house is said to have made a conquest at court that placed, as they say, horns on her husband's head and a medallion on his breast."

"That must be Lady Drat! She is absolutely brazen!" cried Lady Mantiss.

"Oh, I just don't see it," said Vadney. "She's hardly the King's type. And the OMG isn't that hard to get, anyway. My father had one."

"Have you one, Lord Poon-Grebe?" drawled Lord Sauvignon.

"Well, no, but that's hardly . . . I mean, I haven't really . . . it wouldn't . . ."

"I think it's far more likely to be Lady Eldred," Lady Sauvignon said. "She is an ambitious one, and from what I've heard of Lord Eldred's interests his recent award may not have hurt his pride so much as one might think."

"Eldred has an OMG, as well?" Vadney asked. "You see? They really are passing them around to almost anyone, these days."

"Almost," said Lord Sauvignon.

"Great, great stuff," said Sludge.

"I think that should be quite enough, Ratch" Lady Poon-Grebe said, with some steel. "Mistress Blatatat was quite clear that we are here as a resource to her, a well from which she may, perhaps must, draw upon. Who knows what cost there may be or to whom if we squander our attention or energy on this petty chatter and salacious speculation?"

"I think Lady Poon-Grebe is right," said Cyril, worry evident on this face. "I've seen Ekaterina at work many times but it has never been like this. If she needs us we should be ready, somehow."

Ratch nodded, and the group assumed a collective solemnity, one second after Sludge whispered to the manservant, "Let's you and me talk, later."

"Your son, the marquis?"

"Yes, my son, Vadney, the marquis."

Again, the other Poon-Grebes found reason to inspect some fascinating aspect of their garments or the architecture or some something off in the absolutely compelling anywhere-but-hereness.

"Mistress Blatatat, I was and am fond of my son. But the sad fact is that he is an absolutely terrible marquis."

"My lord, forgive me, but I do not understand. My first-hand familiarity with the roles and responsibilities of noblemen and women is meagre. I could not judge."

"Take our word for it, then" boomed Leslie Poon-Grebe. "He is a prodigious nitwit."

"Yes, well, but, be that as it may, your

lordship, I do not see how the current, that is, the living Lord Poon-Grebe's abilities . . ."

"Lack thereof!"

"OK, yes . . . have brought me here, or what bearing it has on my charge to attend to Lord Nelson."

"I do sympathize with your confusion," said Lord Hilary. "I will be direct: We require that my son, Vadney, renounce his marquisate and turn it over to Nelson, of whom we have hope of greater things."

"To Lord Nelson? But he is insensate!"

"Yes. But, as I said, that was our doing. We, shall we say, borrowed him for a time during our decision making."

"I would not presume to question your judgment on this matter, your lordships, but it was my understanding that even prior to his, uh, visit with you, Lord Nelson was . . .

highly individual."

"Indeed, he is! It is for those very qualities we have such hopes. Though not a blood descendent, he has the Poon-Grebe name and an indomitable spirit! How else would one contend so mightily with that mother of his?"

"And have you heard the boy scream?" asked Lord Leslie. "It's terrifying! Really marvelous."

"I see," said Ekaterina, which was mostly a lie. "But what is it that I am doing?"

"You are serving as ambassador, if you will. None of the others have the sensitivities required to come to us, and we thought it undignified to go to them and ghost it up. Plus, we find them tedious in the extreme and would really rather not spend time with them. So, we found this plan more appealing. It's a kind of diplomatic mission you're on."

"But I can't imagine that your son is going to be pleased with this idea, at all. What if he refuses?"

"You will inform him that the diplomatic solution was not the first proposed, nor the most popular."

"Direct him to my portrait and I'll talk to him myself, if he'd like," yelled Lord Leslie.

"And what of Lady Poon-Grebe? I believe she has plans of her own for Lord Nelson."

"I feel certain that the elevation of her son to this position will be sufficient to change her mind. But there is for her an added incentive: You will also make clear to those concerned that Vadney's abdication of his position will be made quite physical by his vacating the family seat. He is to leave Castle Grundel, where Nelson will continue to reside and be educated in a way fitting for the new Marquis d'Isle d'Eaux. That is to say, by his predecessors. By us."

"But you said you would return him!"

"Yes, of course. Never fear, Mistress, Nelson will be returned quite unharmed to the land of, as it's called, the living."

"How then will you deliver his tutelage," Ekaterina pleaded.

"Oh, we won't. You will."

"But that's not how it's done! It's not traditional! It's not proper! It can't be legal! It's not fair!"

The present Marquis d'Isle d'Eaux's voice rose from indignant to strained to whine, as his companions sat in varying degrees of slack-jawedness.

Ekaterina, finally seated and clearly spent, responded limply, "I cannot say if it is proper, legal or fair. Only that your ancestors, a formidable panel, were resolute and that they, at any rate, regard this plan as settled and non-negotiable."

"And Nelson will be as he was?" asked Lady Poon-Grebe.

"Nelson will soon arise, Lady Poon-Grebe. He is, I'm assured, unharmed and healthy, despite recent appearance. Their lordships, in fact, believe that he has rather more promise than any — save your ladyship, of course — ever knew. But I cannot say that he, or anything else, will be the 'same as ever.' That seems unlikely."

"Pardon my thickness, but can I just run through this one more time to see if I follow?" said Cyril. "Would no one mind?"

No one minded.

"So, the previous and deceased dozen Marquises d'Isle d'Eaux, perceiving some promise or purpose in young Nelson, have determined and insisted that he, rather than our present host, should continue that noble function, starting, sort of, now-ish?"

"That is correct."

" And further, the current, or most recent — sorry, my lord — marquis will renounce not only title but ancestral accommodation, as well?"

"Yes. That was quite clear."

"And in his assumption of both duty and domicile, the new marquis is to be accompanied by his mother and instructed by the aforementioned spectral entities via resident proxy — namely, Mistress Ekaterina Blatatat, formerly of the Sink, Boyledin, Maybia?"

"Those are the wishes of their lordships."

Lord Mantiss spoke tentatively, "I'm not quite sure that dead people are supposed to be so directly involved in noble succession. Well, I mean, beyond the actual dying part." He looked to his wife.

With a furrowed brow, she spoke slowly. "I, too, am troubled by this break with precedent. And, yet, none can argue that the Poon-Grebe family has heretofore been an emblem of Maybian accomplishment and dignity. For all the irregularity of its origin, there is some marked merit to the succession. Young Lord Nelson's selection by the cream of our nation's heroes speaks volumes of his eventual character; and even as unproven it could hardly be a poor trade for what has been proven."

Vadney whimpered a thin protest.

The Vicomte de Louche said, more earnestly than was his habit, "I will every day thank Fortune that I am Puissian and not Maybian. You are all so duty-wracked.

What is the point of nobility if it is to be so solemn, so functional? One might as well be a baker or a bailiff. I hardly see what is being lost by our Lord Poon-Grebe."

"Well, there's status, privilege, power and wealth," Sludge piped up, helpfully.

"Wealth?!" both Vadney and Cyril howled in unison, though Cyril retained his seat more easily.

Lady Sauvignon asked, "Do you bake, Lord Poon-Grebe? You don't strike me as a bailiff type."

It was now only by evident effort that Vadney managed to not slide to the floor.

Ekaterina's input was therefore timely and merciful. "You are not to be paupered, Lord Poon-Grebe. Be of calm mind on that. Your predecessors feel that it would be unseemly for a Poon-Grebe to toil, and there was some, um, befuddlement as to what labor, precisely, might best encompass your . . ."

"His lordship's refined temperament and specialized skills," Cyril contributed.

"Yes. Exactly so. Provided you abide by the strictures already identified, namely the abandonment of the marquisate, the appointment of your step-son as your successor and your departure from Castle Grundel, ample wealth is to be arranged."

"Them who gots, gets," muttered Sludge, as Vadney pooled into a puddle of velvet finery atop his own handcrafted shoes.

The Jakes & Japes boiled, burbled and belched with its customary gusto. Grub was grubbed, drinks were drunk. Dolly and her crew muscled through the throng, delivering trenchers, tankards and the occasional tooth from the mouths of the too boldly familiar. Apprentice inebriates ogled the experts till their wills or livers gave out; the experts indulged the attention till their admirers's wallets gave out. Bevis Thrunt ran his tiny furtive eyes over the action — the flow of fare outward, the collection of funds inward — performing rapid calculations luridly.

At the center of this renowned ruckus a quartet of tipplers hunched forward over their drinks in earnest conversation. In another setting the disparity of their social classes might be striking, but in the Jakes & Japes it was not at all unusual to see a man in servant's livery sharing a table with a tradesman, or a tradesman (a journalist, say) with a couple of nobleman. The sharp-eyed observer of this particular group might notice however that one of the two finely dressed men wore his clothes as if entirely new to them. He had difficulty navigating his mug's route from table to mouth without that vessel running aground on the lacy reefs at his wrists and throat consistently. Even one not quite so attuned to the hazards of haberdashery might note that this same gentleman bore a striking resemblance to the more modestly attired Cyril Shakewit, a previous regular of the tavern and staple of its Amateur Recitation Night, which was currently unfolding onstage without the slightest interest by this be-doilied doppelgänger. But, of course, sharp eyes were in short supply on the soberest of nights at the J&J and the alcoholic apparatus of Amateur Recitation Night has been well documented. We will not dawdle here to recapitulate its high-octane economic elegance and will instead give our attention to our egalitarian conversationalists.

"Well, I'd hardly call it a nightmare, my lord."

"Wouldn't you, Cyril? Is it not nightmarish to have the ghosts of your ancestors assembled, en masse, to tell you, in company, that you are so profound a disappointment it echoes through ages and pains even the dead? Is it not nightmarish to be told by your Grandpas that you must, on pain of some supernatural consequence, relinquish your hereditary title and forfeit your home to a boy still perched, as it were, on his mother's bony lap, and must slink off shamefully with only the clothes on your back?"

"There you have it, my lord! In my nightmares I'm always naked as an ape! This is much nicer than that! Though I could do with less of this dratted lace in my drink."

"And, sir, I did take the liberty of contacting your tailor in town. A full wardrobe should arrive at the house here, presently. Shall I dispense with last season's garments?"

"Oh, I don't care, Ratch. Do whatever we usually do with them. Or have the lace shortened and give them to Cyril. Or Sludge, you take them and distribute them among your lot. Why are journalists so consistently terribly dressed, by the way?"

"It's our perverse natures, I suspect, sir. Plain spite."

"Yes, well, in any event, it's not the bare

facts of it all. It's the principle."

"Lord Poon-Grebe, without attempting to diminish your appropriate surprise at this unexpected turn, I would like to examine for a moment just those: the bare facts."

"What? And to itemize, articulate and relive the insults against me, Cyril?"

"No, I don't think so, my lord. Attend, if you will: What was it you most hoped for as a result of Mistress Blatatat's efforts? Your independence from Lady Poon-Grebe and Nelson. You have most decidedly attained that."

"But I've lost my castle in the process!"

"True. But observe: I have before me a mug brimming with a delightfully intoxicating concoction. I am quite fond of it. Now, take it away from me."

"I don't want it, Cyril. I have my own — and I'm sure that yours tastes of wrist and neck, besides."

"You don't have to drink it, just take it."

Vadney complied, albeit with stagy and only barely tolerant indulgence, and Cyril pivoted and deftly swiped a full mug from the loaded tray of a passing wench (who did not slow for a moment, confident that the all-seeing accountant's eye of Thrunt would tally and tabulate with eerie precision). Cyril placed the drink in the center of the table and gestured to it theatrically.

"Ta-da!"

Vadney looked upon Cyril in exasperated perplexity. He turned to Sludge and Ratch, whose expressions were, if not entirely clear to him, clearly less exasperatedly perplexed than he had had hoped.

" 'Ta-da?' What was the point of that?"

Cyril swiveled and grabbed yet another drink. And another. (Across the room Bevis

Thrust adjusted his garments and dabbed at his brow.)

"Lord Poon-Grebe, you have lost a home and gained a horizon! The one place denied you is now also the one place to which, by title, responsibility, tradition and ghostly ancestral decree, your wife and step-son are most positively, procedurally, publicly bound!"

Recognition and understanding broke slow as Flenish morning across Vadney's face. His brow raised, his eyes shone, his lips twitched like fishes hooked by his hair. He very nearly beamed. But it all fell floorward in an instant.

"But castles aren't paraded about by serving wenches for the grabbing, Cyril."

(At the syntactical placement of "grabbing" so close by "serving wenches" Cyril and Sludge, the party's most regular

J&J patrons, reflexively flinched. But they did not interrupt.)

"And to have been turned away, rejected by my family . . . I am disgraced, scandalized! Word spreads quickly among noble families. When Lord whatsisname was discovered to have, what was it, Ratch? A secret harem of pot-bellied women in the New World, or something . . ."

"It was, sir, the Duke of Catwalk who was reputed to have fathered a small tribe of giantesses during his campaign in the Giselles."

"Yes, yes. Whatever is was, it spread like the pox. It was all people talked about that season."

"But Lord Poon-Grebe, you are forgetting that we have had all along a secret weapon: the news."

Lord Poon-Grebe followed Cyril's eyes

to Sludge, whose Daisy-froth-flecked mustache indicated more than just his usual self-satisfaction.

"It ain't boasting to admit that Cyril's hit it on the head, my lord," the newspaperman crowed. " 'Cause it ain't just me and my instincts and my way with words. If there were a dozen of me I couldn't keep up with the need. You might think it was just the commoners who hang on the every word of the early, mid-day and late editions. But you should see the servants scurrying to get the papers back to the finest estates soon as the hawkers cut the bundles. It's a frenzy."

"Yes, fine. But how does that help me? You're saying that word of my shame will spread even faster and farther than I feared?"

"Mitch, do you have any copies of your recent work about you?"

"Why, I most certainly do, Cyril. I am most scrupulous about the maintenance of my archive. And I do dearly love rereading my words."

"Would you, then, be so kind as to share with us a selection of your most recent headlines, from the relevant dispatches?"

"With both pride and pleasure!"

Sludge cleared his throat and recited, in all caps:

POON-GREBE PRE-TEEN PARALYZED BY UNSEEN!

ELDRITCH ACOLYTE TO ATTEND ARISTO HEIR!

SWELLS SUMMONED TO SUPERNATURAL SUMMIT!

❊ ❊ ❊

THE UNKNOWN GRUNDEL: TORTURE BENEATH THE TURRETS!

I AM A TYPICAL NOVICE AT OUR LADY OF ECSTATIC MORTIFICATION . . .

Sludge paused and shuffled the papers he had pulled from his coat pocket. "Wait. That's something I'm working on privately. Ah, here!"

"MAD, BAD," SAYS MARQUIS'S DEAD DAD!

He concluded his recital and passed the clips to Vadney, who skimmed them each in turn.

"You have made me sound like a dangerous lunatic!" he cried out.

"Oh, absolutely," said Sludge. "Readers are going completely mental for it. Circulation has simply exploded. Haven't seen anything like this since the Maurice Sons' drowning. Bloody wonderful."

"But I'm barely recognizable! This Vadney Poon-Grebe makes the first marquis seem like . . . well, like Vadney Poon-Grebe!"

"If you would, your lordship, one more time, humor me," Cyril coaxed. "Go take a drink."

Vadney had no energy left to contend with Cyril. He turned on his bench looking for a passing tray, but Cyril said, "No, Lord Poon-Grebe. That drink."

Vadney traced the length of Cyril's extended arm and forefinger and the implied ray beyond. It intersected quite inarguably with a mass so great as to seem only possibly, but not likely, human.

"You're joking."

"Trust me."

In future, Vadney was never able to recall this moment clearly. Was there a sudden presence within him, some previously unknown courage? Or did he remember a sudden emptiness, a rush of departing sense, wisdom or a will to live unmangled? But stand he did, and walk he did, and full mug from behemoth seize he did.

When he returned, pale but unpummeled, to rest the drink on the table, he was at first unable to speak, or perhaps to hear. Cyril repeated the question:

"What happened, my lord?"

"I told that enormous person that I would have his drink."

"And then?"

"And then he growled, I suppose you would call it, and started to rise."

"And then?"

"And then I braced for an intensely awkward reunion with my ancestors."

"And then?"

"And then the other fellow, the littler fellow, laid his hand on the larger fellow's impossible forearm and . . . he said . . ."

"Yes?"

"He said, 'Don't be daft, man. Don't you know who that is?'"

Vadney drained the mug in a single gulp.

Lord Vadney Kimberly Carroll Poon-Grebe, the former 13th Marquis d'Isle d'Eaux, and Mr. Cyril Shakewit, former resident of the Sink, Boyledin, Maybia, stood at the rail of the sailing ship "Lucky

II" (so named as a tribute to its predecessor, the unnumbered "Lucky," which had mysteriously exploded).

The men were buffeted by wind and cold spray but were, themselves, bright and cheerful — or at least animated by the type of naive uncertainty subtle wits term "optimism."

"I am still amazed at the rapidity and reach of the popular press," Lord Poon-Grebe was saying. "I admit that I was unaware of its growth even in our own land and so perhaps it's no surprise to find new revelations about my ignorance. But for word to have reached so far as the Orals! And come to think of it, are the Maybian papers translated for foreign readers? Does the *Fervid Inquisitor* have a Vladistanian edition?"

"I admit that I have no idea, myself. But

the Zamfirs are a worldly family, my lord. If I remember correctly, your correspondent was himself educated in Maybia. Not unusual for the better families from the remote regions."

"Remote? Yes, that's a delicate enough word for it: on the slopes of the most imposing mountain of the most treacherous range in the most legendarily cruel backwater of the central continent!"

"It's a testament to the worthiness of the approach, my lord, when the results are surprising to even its architects."

"Yes, I suppose, Cyril. I'm coming to take your word on such things. I do wish though that we knew more. Or that Ratch's knowledge of the peculiarities and peccadillos of the nobility extended somewhat farther east."

"We can't begrudge him his patriotic

emphases of expertise. And certainly they will serve him well in his new venture."

"Indeed. And I wish him only well. Both of them. What did Sludge call it? *Access Aristocracy*? Still, I'd feel surer with a more complete understanding of what we're heading into."

"What's to wonder, my lord? Zeno Zamfir, only son and heir to the Black Saint of the White Mountain, seeks to preserve his family's reputation during his father's — uh — his father's hiatus. What better place to start than a little dungeon upgrade and consult from the notorious Mad Marquis?"

The Mad Marquis turned toward the prow, staring across the channel, across the country yet to cross, into the bleak, steep central continent, into the fabled realm of perversion ancient and unchanging after eras, up the uncivilized slopes of the Orals, up the fearsome serrated ridges of Albamonte.

"Do you think it's really that simple, Cyril?"

"Almost certainly not, my lord. Almost certainly not."

Made in the USA
Columbia, SC
23 April 2018